Detective LaFleur Mysteries
by
Steve Abbott and John Fountain

O.R.

Firesign

HOT GOLD

A Detective LaFleur Mystery

Steve Abbott

John Fountain

This is a work of fiction. Names, characters, places, and incidents are the product of the authors' imaginations or are used fictitiously. Any resemblance to actual events, locales, or persons, living or dead, is entirely coincidental.

ISBN-13: 978-1492775959
ISBN-10: 1492775959

Copyright © 2013 by Steven Abbott and John Fountain

To family and friends, both here and absent

Nonbeing must in some sense be, otherwise what is it that there is not? This tangled doctrine might be nicknamed *Plato's beard*; historically it has proved tough, frequently dulling the edge of Occam's razor.

-- Willard Van Orman Quine

HOT GOLD

Prologue: What's That Noise?

Armand Broussard was just dropping off to sleep, book falling from his hands, when he was startled awake by a noise from the back room of his small jewelry shop, which was located directly below his apartment.

He'd come home late from a selling trip to Toronto, where he'd planned to stay overnight, but his client had called and cancelled just as he'd rounded the end of Lake Ontario, heading north. The unexpected drive back to Oswego in the dark had worn him out. He usually dealt with a jeweler in Kingston, a small city just over the Canadian border, almost directly north of Oswego, across the lake. But the money in Toronto was usually good, so it was hard to turn down, even given the inconvenience. He much preferred going to Kingston on business; it was more than two hours closer, and a prettier drive.

Armand laid the book on the bedside table and settled back into his pillow, closing his eyes but leaving the light on, listening. Even though it had been two years since his wife Anne-Marie had died, he was still not used to living alone. He'd sold the house and moved into the vacant apartment above the shop just a couple of months after her death. His daughter Karin had warned him at the time that he was making the decision too soon. He was loathe to admit she may have been right, especially since his son Jacques—who had insisted on being known as "Jimmy" as soon as he got to junior high school—had also advised him against moving in. In Jimmy's case, however, it was that he'd had his eye on it for himself. Always on the lookout for a free ride.

Armand had long ago given up trying to understand how it was his two children had grown up to be such different people: Karin, quiet, strong and compassionate, a nurse; Jimmy, loud, brash, irresponsible, usually unemployed, this close to jail. Armand's aunt Louise had long ago told him her reason for having multiple children—if they all turn out different, it proves that a problem child wasn't your fault.

Armand had also given up on any thought of Jimmy taking over the business. He had to admit that Oswego, New York was not exactly the jewelry capital of the East; but even so, Armand's business was fairly lucrative. And with gold prices soaring, he had also built up a small scrap gold business. It hadn't happened overnight, and it wasn't a simple matter of just sitting back and watching gold walk in the front door. There was a lot of competition. Fortunately he'd made quite a good connection in Kingston, which had an active scrap jewelry market, though it had taken two years to get together all the customs documentation that made it worthwhile.

It was only after he started living alone, above the store, that he began hearing noises in the middle of the night. The shop had never been burglarized, not in all the thirty-one years he'd been in business, but lately, with the price of gold at astronomical levels, and crime rates to match, Broussard imagined a break-in with every late night disturbance. He nervously investigated each and every time, never finding anything amiss. The cat, dog, raccoon, owl—whatever had caused the racket—was, as usual, long gone by the time he made it downstairs and through the shop to the location of the noise. Occasionally he spied a dark streak taking off down the alley after he went through to the back and opened the outer door.

There it was again.
Louder this time.
He swung out of bed and into his slippers, cautiously

made his way to the stairs, and crept down to the shop as quietly as he could. He asked himself for the hundredth time why he always forced himself to go downstairs, undressed and unarmed, illogically not trusting the alarm to have been triggered in the case of an actual break-in. He'd had CCTV cameras installed, and even had a monitor in the apartment, but they'd been on the fritz again. Need to get those fixed.

He paused at the bottom of the stairs and told himself again: if for some inexplicable reason the alarm hadn't gone off—and he tested it regularly—what did he think he could do if there really was something wrong?

Streetlight coming in through the front window faintly illuminated the long display cases, the rows of watch bands, rings, pendants, and gold chains glistening in the dark. This made it possible for him to work his way carefully towards the rear of the showroom without turning on a light.

Maybe I *should* get a gun, he thought as he moved slowly in the increasingly dim light towards the backroom. But he just wasn't the type, he quickly told himself, as always. He understood why most of the other jewelers he knew were armed in one way or another—many kept more than one gun close at hand—but Broussard just couldn't bring himself to do it. It was not necessarily an ethical or moral issue—he believed he had every right to defend himself in any way necessary were he attacked, or burglarized. No, it was more of a cultural issue, he believed. His father, a fourth-generation French-Canadian, a true Québécois, had instilled in him a formidable set of old world values. As had the priest at the St. Louis cathedral. "Packing heat" was not a respectable way to live. Even though he *was* an American now, and when living in certain areas and working in some professions…and as times change…maybe…

He stopped as he reached the rear wall of the shop.

There was no light showing from under the door.

He stood there a moment, scarcely breathing, listening intently. He heard soft scuffling noises coming from behind the door. *I should just call 9-1-1*, he thought nervously as he turned the knob, pushing his way into the room as the door creaked open.

He stopped just inside the door, momentarily confused by what he saw—was there something moving in the dark? He couldn't make it out, couldn't process what was happening quickly enough to make sense of it. A bat?

"What?" he said, unconsciously, turning in the doorway, groping along the wall for the light switch with one hand, steadying himself against the doorframe with the other. He heard something behind him. Movement, a quick peripheral vision of a large, shapeless form, caused him to jerk his head sideways. A brief flash of panic constricted his chest. He gasped.

This time, there was no stray cat to chase away, no clang of a trash can lid, an urbanized red fox vixen searching for food for its kits. No, this time, Armand Broussard had been right.

Switching on the light was the last thing he ever did.

Doctor's Corner

The new owner of the 1850 House Restaurant and Bar stepped back to admire the freshly painted name in the front window: *A.C. LaFleur, Proprietor.*

Proprietor. A grand word. A word with a pedigree, a word with heft. It echoed LaFleur's deep-seated beliefs in the propriety of personal responsibility—and the necessity of taking a proprietary role in a new endeavor, something to renew and rebuild his life. Yes, "proprietor" sounds pretty good. Not necessarily *better* than "ex-detective," he told himself, but that particular role had been bringing him nothing but trouble for the past two years. Now he was, at long last, after an already long-seeming retirement, looking forward to doing something new, yet still satisfying. And less dangerous.

It had been just six months since the boat he'd been living on had been transformed into a burned-out hulk, now mired in the mud at the bottom of the Port Authority marina, blown up by a pyromaniac's attack. He'd barely escaped with his—and his cat Newton's—life. He'd been investigating a cold case at the request of his close friend Maggie Malone, a retired nurse. A young SUNY coed had died after being seriously burned in an apartment fire, a fire which everyone except the local police department knew to be arson; Maggie had treated her at the Clarke burn unit in Syracuse. It had all ended in nightmarish irony as he watched the murderess deliberately set herself on fire in a fraternity house kitchen.

He shook off the chill that had suddenly started to set in

as the cars on Bridge Street swept past, but it was a chill caused more by the thought of that investigation than by the early fall air. He turned and went back inside, walked over to his favorite table, known as the "Doctor's Corner," and sat down and looked around. A small sideboard near the table was still decorated with a few antique medical instruments, reminding him of the many hours he'd spent sitting at this table with his friends Dr. Michael Fuentes and Maggie, discussing the details of another case of Maggie's—the alleged suicide, by anesthesia, of a young nurse at Oswego Hospital. Another cold case—forty years cold—had nonetheless become a murder investigation.

Seemed like no matter where he looked, there was another reminder—like the small wooden case on the sideboard containing some large, glass syringes. That brought back the hard truth that their actions had nearly led to Maggie's death at the hand of a major suspect, for which LaFleur blamed himself. He caught his reflection in the glass of a small display case holding a variety of antique surgical instruments—a strong, well-featured face, even if a little "gaunt," Maggie had said, but still relatively unlined; swept back gray hair, just recently starting to thin; and clear, steel-gray eyes behind his glasses.

LaFleur got up and went back to the bar, brooding all the way, his bright morning outlook in danger of fading into remorse. The final resolution of the nurse's death had been in a conventional sense less than satisfying, the probable killer either dead or simply vanished, never brought to strict justice—bureaucratic justice, at least. Which in many ways was preferable, LaFleur believed, to the long, drawn out and ultimately futile prospect of putting someone in jail (assuming a conviction, never guaranteed no matter the evidence, in his experience), and all done at the taxpayer's expense, with no restitution to the victim. The only clear advantage of incarceration he could see was the inability of the criminal to commit another crime while actually in prison—in theory, at least—and only then until a parole or an early release "put them back out on the streets," as the saying went, often coming out with a new criminal skill set. Prison was nothing more than "crime vo-tech," LaFleur maintained.

With the purchase of the 1850 House, which had closed down the year before, LaFleur had his own place again, the apartment over the restaurant. He'd been living with Maggie in Syracuse since he'd lost the boat, but now he was able to return the favor by giving her a place to live—permanently, he hoped.

The insurance settlement on his boat had provided the seed money for the venture. The 1850 House bar had been one of LaFleur's favorite haunts for years, and with the recent demise of his alternate home away from home, Patz on the River, he saw more in this endeavor than just an opportunity to get into a new business—he could restore to Oswego a much needed community resource. With Maggie to take care of the finances, and an old friend, "Big Frank" Ivanovich managing the kitchen, all that was left for LaFleur was the bar. It was turning out to be the perfect retirement gig.

And to top it off, now he got his Scotch wholesale.

Jimmy and the 'krainians

Jimmy Broussard sat at the bar in the Port Tavern swilling his beer. That's exactly the mood he was in tonight, just sitting there, "swilling." He was dressed for the part; greasy jeans, scuffed leather coat, his skinny legs and arms barely filling either.

He sat there, swilling, feeling sorry for himself. Nothing he'd tried lately had paid off, not a thing. That he had not actually expended any real effort in trying to make something legitimate pay off didn't occur to him. Always looking for the easy money, the quick hit. He dimly recognized that as a personal failing at times like this, sitting alone in the bar, swilling, waiting for someone to come along with an easy out. *I'm a pig,* he thought, *a swilling pig. Swilling pig.* That makes a good curse, he thought, brightly. I'm going to use that. "You swilling pig!" he'd say. "Fedir Bondurenko, you swilling pig!" That goddam 'krainian wouldn't have a clue what it meant. That was good. He couldn't wait.

They were supposed to be here by now.

"Shit, shit, shit," he said, leaning over and thumping his forehead on the bar, his long, dark hair spreading out in a ragged fan on each side of his head, skinny elbows spread out like chicken wings. Dewey, the bar's current permanent stool fixture, raised his head up from the sticky counter where it usually rested, and said, with as much consternation as he could manage, "What?"

Jimmy turned his head and peered at Dewey from bar level, through some stray strands of hair. Not a good angle.

"Go back to sleep, Dewey." Dewey obliged.

Lifting his head, Jimmy sat up and looked around carefully, as if hoping to make some sense of his world. The world that had been closing in on him slowly for the past few months. Ever since he'd gotten hooked up with those damn 'krainians. Well, even before that, he had to admit. It wasn't the Bondurenkos fault. Karin, after all, had been the one who had introduced him to Valentyn Bondurenko—and Val and Karin were still seeing one another. Appeared to be getting pretty serious, as far as Jimmy knew. Of course, he didn't talk to Karin that much.

Val had asked Jimmy to meet him here, he was pretty sure. He looked at his watch. Val had said he was interested in the jewelry business.

They were supposed to have been here by now.

Hours ago.

Jimmy took a drink.

Val had taken Jimmy home more than once after a hard night of him trying to keep up with him and Fedir. They'd spent a lot time here, making plans. That's why he was here, to make some new plans, to talk to Val about the scrap gold business, the Canada connection, that's what Val had said, important stuff. But nothing to worry about, nothing complicated, Val had said. Jimmy, he would be a facilitator. That's all Uncle Lev had asked for, just help out with some minor details.

Where the hell were they?

"You swilling pig, Freddy," he suddenly said out loud, and laughed, snorting, making Dewey look up again.

"Hey, Dewey." Dewey slumped back down. Jimmy dejectedly swilled the last dregs of his beer. He wasn't as drunk as he'd hoped to be by now.

Shit. He held up his bottle in the general direction of the bartender, the universal sign for one more, although Jimmy knew how to order another beer in about ten different languages. *Uno mas, por favor. Mō ippon, kudasai. Ein andere, bitte*. Might come in handy someday, he thought. He'd tried to learn the Ukrainian from Val—*meni, bud' laska pyva*—but so far could remember only "bud." Which in spite of how it sounded, didn't even *mean* beer, as far as he could tell.

***

When Val and Freddy finally showed up, about two hours late, Jimmy was impersonating Dewey, head on the bar, not quite asleep, but far from fully conscious. The bartender had cut him off an hour ago. In fact, Dewey'd had the good sense to wake up and go home, while Jimmy sat and drank.

Val and Fedir walked him around outside for a few minutes trying to clear his head before they sat down to talk. As it turned out, Jimmy was a little too far gone to be useful.

"*Pah*," said Fedir. "We are wasting time here."

Val had to agree.

"Sorry we were late, Jimmy boy; couldn't be helped." Jimmy gazed blearily into Val's face.

"S'no problem, Val. I wasn't doing anything anyway."

"We'd still like to get together to discuss the business."

"Sure, sure," Jimmy said, waving his arms expansively. "Any time."

"Great, Jimmy. I think it's about time you met our Uncle Lev."

A Damn Good Chicken Spiedie

Jimmy had to knock twice to be heard over the noise coming from within the house; it sounded like there was quite a large gathering. After waiting a minute or so, trying to decide whether or not to knock again, the door suddenly opened. A bullet-headed, swarthy character in a dark suit motioned him in.

"Who?" Bullet Head asked bluntly.

"Um, Jimmy, uh, Broussard. Jimmy Broussard. I'm here to see—"

"Wait."

Jimmy wiped his hands on his jeans nervously as he waited, looking through the entry way into a large living room, trying to see how everyone else was dressed. At least he'd put on a sport coat, he thought with some relief, as the guests he saw were dressed somewhat more formally.

Bullet Head came back into the foyer and motioned for Jimmy to follow him. Winding their way through several clumps of guests, Jimmy was finally deposited at the bar near the rear of the house. His escort tapped a short, stocky man dressed in a very nice suit on the shoulder, saying in a low murmur, "Lev. Jimmy."

The man at the bar turned towards Jimmy.

"Ah. *Bitajemo*, Jimmy. Welcome to my home." The man stuck his hand out.

"Thank you very much, Mr. Bondurenko."

"Ah, call me *dyad'ko*," Lev said expansively, shaking Jimmy's hand.

"Uh, 'Dave-ko?'"

"Or for you, maybe better in English: 'Uncle.' Uncle Lev. Uncle Lev, the Lion!" He laughed loudly, clapping Jimmy on the shoulder. "Lev, it means 'lion' in Ukrainian," Lev explained helpfully.

"Okay, sure," Jimmy stammered, "Lev. Okay!"

Standing nearby watching this exchange was Lev's nephew Valentyn Bondurenko. Known to Jimmy as "Val," he had brought Jimmy out to the party at Lev's house near Pulaski in order to introduce him. He hoped it was not going to turn out to be a mistake.

Lev, however expansive his personality, was not an equally imposing figure physically. Jimmy—his knowledge based solely on the stereotypical Russian as portrayed in B movies—had expected a large, bear-like man with a big black mustache and arms like Smithfield hams: Stalinesque, intimidating. Lev was actually only Jimmy's height, even slightly under, about five-nine, with a fine-featured square face and thick, black hair, combed straight back, slightly grey on the sides, at the roots. No mustache. With the exception of the black hair, Jimmy saw a resemblance to Val.

"Jimmy's going to be our 'man in the know,' around town" Val said to Lev, using an American expression he'd just picked up from a thriller on TBS the night before.

"*Tak*, yes. Very good," Lev said approvingly. "We don't know all of the right people here," he said. "Valentyn tells me, Jimmy, well, Jimmy knows everyone, right? Jimmy, he is the Man In The Know," he repeated stiffly in his heavy accent, also proud to learn new idioms.

"This is a very nice house, Mr. Bondurenko," Jimmy said, looking around, taking in the huge bar, the swimming pool just outside the patio doors, the view out across Lake Ontario, the boat dock. He had driven through the golf course on the way in. "You've, uh, done very well for yourself here in New York."

"Land of Opportunity," Lev said, spreading his arms wide, sounding to Jimmy's uncultured ears more like "Lund ov ope-ee-*tayr*-nee-tee."

"Come," Lev said, taking Jimmy by the arm and leading him to the bar. "You must have drinks. Something to eat. We have very good spiedie, I make it myself. Special marinade." *Mah-ree-nada.* Val, standing slightly behind Lev, caught Jimmy's eye and winked. "So, some good food, some good drink, then later we talk, okay? Okay." He walked away, already smiling and waving to some newcomers across the room.

"Lev always serves chicken spiedie sandwiches at his parties," Val said. "He likes to adopt the local customs wherever he goes. He's very good at it. He had his first chicken spiedie at a little dockside place up at Sandy Point when he first moved here. He loved it, and now he serves them all the time."

Hell, Jimmy thought to himself, scooping some of the marinated chicken onto a bun, a spiedie was Italian, not Russian, or Ukrainian, whatever. And biting into it, he had to admit it was a damn good spiedie.

No Problemo

Lev entered the library, closing the door behind him, and sat down behind his desk. Val and Jimmy had been waiting for him, seated in two large chairs in front of the desk.

As in all things Lev did, he had gone overboard on the library. He'd hired a "library consultant," he explained proudly. The consultant had created a library suitable not for reading—there were no Russian or Ukrainian books on the shelves, for example—but for impressing guests. Many leather bound, special editions, pretty but cheap, auction items, mainly; early turn of the century bindings that looked impressive but were literally a dime a dozen, multi-volume, outdated histories, collected works of once-popular authors who were for good reason long forgotten, fancy-looking book club editions. A smattering of literary works in expensive bindings rounded it out. The consultant had also suggested leaving a few areas of shelf space open in order to display the occasional *objet d'art*, of which Lev had a large number: wooden eggs painted with religious scenes (called *Pysanky,* Lev told Jimmy); colorfully decorated plates; a few Matryoshka nesting dolls, subtly different from their Russian counterparts, not truly a Ukrainian art form, but Lev had them there because everyone expected to see one; and hand-carved and painted wooden dolls. All first class, no cheap souvenirs or reproductions, Lev was careful to point out. Leather arm chairs and an antique smoking stand completed the effect.

"So, the jewelry business is very interesting" Lev said, after he'd allowed time for Jimmy to admire the library sufficiently. "I like jewelry." He held up his hands, showing Jimmy a large gold signet ring on each hand. "Very nice, yes?" he asked. One ring was embossed with some foreign language symbols—Jimmy guessed it was the Russian alphabet—and the other had the head of a lion carved into it, with strong, dark lines marking the mane surrounding a stern lion's face, head on.

"Yes, very," Jimmy said.

Lev turned his hands around and admired his rings for a moment, then put them back down on the desk. "I am interested in doing some jewelry business with your father. Can you help me with that, Jimmy?"

After some hesitation, Jimmy nodded and said yes. Lev did not hear the enthusiasm he would have liked to have heard in Jimmy's voice.

"You know the business, you work with your father, yes?" he pressed.

"Not exactly," Jimmy admitted. "We haven't been getting along lately."

Lev glanced at Val as he confirmed Jimmy's meaning. "You don't work with your father in the business?" he asked. This would never happen in Ukraine.

"I did, yeah, for a while. Until about two years ago, when we had a problem. But anyway, yeah, my old man, he always wanted me to take over the business for him, you know? But, I don't know, it's just too, well, too *straight* for me, know what I mean? I guess it's a great jewelry store; people have been going to him for years, repeat customers, so it must be good, right? It's a very classy shop, and he runs it the good old-fashioned way. Even still uses an old-style loupe, one that just clips to his head? Anyway, he's very popular around town, too. People trust him. I guess that's how he's built up the used gold trade, too, even though it's not his main business. I think he makes a lot more selling rings and watches than he makes buying and selling the gold. 'Slag,' he calls it sometimes."

"What is this, this *slag*?" asked Lev.

"Um, that's just what he calls the scrap jewelry, the gold he buys and sells. He has a guy in Canada he deals with all the time; I was telling Val about it." Val nodded to Lev; he'd told him about it earlier. It was why Jimmy was here.

"Can you tell me more about that, Jimmy? He takes it into Canada? Why is that?" Lev asked.

"Yeah," Jimmy said, "like, he takes the scrap gold to Canada because, one, he can get a better price—I think the guy up there has some arrangement with dealers in the Middle East or something, they have all the money—and two, he can just breeze in and out of the country with almost not even stopping at the border. And not only that, with no tariffs on scrap jewelry, his profit—"

"He breezes in and out?" Lev interrupted. "What means that? I mean," he said, glancing at Val, his English tutor, "What does mean, no, what does *that* mean?"

Jimmy didn't let Val answer. "You know, Lev…Uncle Lev…it's just as easy as pie."

Lev turned, frowning, again turning to Val. "Valentyn, *ya ne rozumiyu*. I do not understand."

"He says it's no problem," Val said, translating Jimmy's colloquialism.

"Ah," said Lev. "I see. Or as they say in the Mexico, '*no problemo*,' eh, Jimmy?"

"Yeah, man. *No problemo*." Jimmy was pretty sure the correct Spanish was "*problema*," but he didn't think this was the right time to point this out.

"So, how does this work, Jimmy?"

The Canadian import program was called FAST, Jimmy then explained—Fast and Secure Trade. The program made it easy for Armand to transport scrap jewelry into Canada. He had a set of bar-coded documents—just flash those at the border, Jimmy said, go right in. Everything else done later. Faster, cheaper. And no tariffs. The FAST pass was also useful as an ID, Jimmy stressed. Val had particularly liked that aspect, being careful not to mention the ease with which documents of this type can be forged (with the right connections, and a good example to work from).

Lev considered the information Jimmy had just provided. "You know a lot about this, Jimmy; I am impressed."

"Well, yeah. Like I said, I used to make some of the Canada trips with him, so I know how it all works." Jimmy said.

"How many trips does he do, how often does he go?" Lev asked.

"Oh, once a month. Pretty regular, he has a guy there, like I said."

"Excellent. Well, Jimmy, we would like to get into the gold business. Take scrap gold to the dealer there, along with the regular gold shipment. Just like you have told us." He paused. "You can help us with this? Arrange it with your father?"

"Sure, I guess so," Jimmy said.

"Good, Jimmy, very good," Lev said. "What is the next time he will go to Canada?"

***

Lev left Val and Jimmy alone in the library, saying he would "catch them up later."

Jimmy was mellow, comfortable, at ease in his new found position of trust. He sat back, raising his glass to Val, and took a sip of vodka.

The library door opened. Jimmy looked up, immediately annoyed at not seeing Lev returning. It was that goddam Fedir, Val's brother—"Freddy," he liked to be called. But no one ever called him that. *He's no "Freddy,"*

Jimmy thought darkly. He was a "Fedir" through and through. Olive-skinned and stocky, muscular, with glossy black hair and an even darker, bristly mustache. Right out of a spy thriller. Jimmy was a little afraid of Fedir.

It was too bad about Fedir, since Val was such a great guy. He looked nothing at all like his brother—fair, light brown hair, cinematically good-looking, much better English than Freddy, or even Lev, for that matter. Nice guy. He was glad Karin had met Val— she was the one who'd introduced him to Jimmy. She'd met Val at the hospital a few months earlier, where he worked as an orderly, and they'd started seeing one another regularly. He didn't know what Karin thought of Fedir, but he would be surprised if it were anything good.

"Jimmy," said Fedir, shortly. He did not like Jimmy.

"Hi, *Fedir*."

Fedir scowled. "I join you, okay?"

Jimmy looked to Val for guidance. Val was already motioning Fedir to an empty arm chair.

"So, Jimmy," Fedir was saying as he settled into his chair, "tell us more about your father's jewelry store."

The vodka flowed.

Jimmy talked.

More vodka.

Fedir kept pouring, small shots, but lots of them. Jimmy couldn't refuse, it would be an insult, he thought, in Lev's house. At the same time Jimmy was learning that the stereotype of the hard-drinking Russian had something to it. Okay, Ukrainian, must be the same thing, all that vodka. And if it wasn't true it wouldn't be a stereotype, right?

Jimmy told them everything.

***

A little later, Val nodded at Jimmy, indicating he'd heard enough. "So, like Lev said, we would like to get into this gold business. We have some items to, to—to sell."

Fedir leaned forward quickly, pointing at Jimmy. "*You* will take gold to Canada for us, yes?" Jimmy shrank back a bit in his chair at Fedir's demand. He was *pretty* sure he could get his father to agree, but still…

Val glanced at Fedir, and then held his hands out to Jimmy in an apologetic gesture. "We are only asking you, Jimmy, if you can please do this for us."

Not wanting to deny Val, Jimmy leaned forward himself, waving a hand in the air. "Sure thing, Val. You bet." He could deal with his father somehow, he was sure.

Val stood up. "So, Jimmy, maybe enough vodka for one night, eh? I think we are done here."

Jimmy nodded, ever agreeable. "Sure, Val. So, you think we can really work something out, then, with Lev and all? Something we can all make some real money on, I mean."

"Oh, yes, Jimmy." As Jimmy stood up he put his arm around his shoulder. "I'm sure we can 'work it out,' as you say. 'We can work it all out,' that is from the Beatles, no?" He sang a bar from the chorus. "We loved the Beatles in Ukraine."

Jimmy beamed. Val was a great guy.

***

Much later, after Jimmy had been sent home in a cab, Lev sat down with Val in the library to discuss some ideas he had been formulating.

"So," Lev began, "this friend Jimmy. He is—ah, reliable? You say, what, 'worth trusting?'"

"Trustworthy. To a point." Val switched to Ukrainian, thinking it would be easier on Lev, and started into a detailed description of what he knew about Jimmy, his father, and his sister Karin, before Lev interrupted him.

"English. Use English. I must, ah, become, better, in my English. People here do not trust someone who does not speak good English. You see this, always in the hospital, yes? The accent, I think that is maybe okay. But the English should still be good."

"Okay, yes, it is important. Maybe you can explain that to Fedir…?" This got only a black look from his brother.

"Fedir is Fedir," said Lev. Fedir looked momentarily confused, frowning as he tried to decipher this, and then shrugged. Must have meant something good, he decided.

"So, anyway," continued Val, "I think this thing Jimmy's father has going could be a good thing for us. He takes this gold to Canada all the time, he's doing it so much, he doesn't think much about it anymore. It would be really easy to get in on the gold business and—"

"Gold. *Pah*. I am not so interested in the gold. The gold that he takes, it is just old rings and bracelets, yes? Just, as you say, scrap?"

"Well, yeah. You heard Jimmy; he says his father even calls it slag, like something you throw away. Except this slag has a lot of value, Lev. The price of gold—"

"Goes up and down. And Jimmy's father, he carries how much gold to Canada? A few grams, maybe half a kilogram, a little more, I don't know, what, a thousand, two thousand dollars? Not worth my time. No, we need Jimmy's father, Armand, for much more than that. We need what he can do for us. To get something special into Canada. Something that will bring us much more money than these little slags, these little bits of gold."

Val waited patiently as Lev went to his desk and got out a yellow legal pad and a pen. As soon as Lev sat back down across from Val, he started writing out a list, talking to himself, *odyn, dva, tri*, until he had five tasks listed.

"Okay," he said, lifting his head up to look at Val and Fedir. "This is what you are going to do."

***

Lev sat on the deck at the back of the house, looking out over the lake. The sun was just coming up; the sky was all the colors it was supposed to be. Like sunrise at the Black Sea, at Zakota. Just like this.

He pulled a cell phone from his coat pocket and dialed.

"Hello, Arkady, it is Lev here. *Tak.* Yes. We can deliver what you want. No, no. Yes, very soon. Soon we will have a, a safe conduct, a safe way. In plenty of time."

He stretched his neck, back and forth, up and down. He rested his head on his hand. It had been a long night. A long time planning, before tonight. Now it was almost time.

"Yes, first we send two grams. You test it. You will see; it is the real thing."

Lev listened for a moment, unconsciously nodding in agreement to whatever was being said at the other end. "Yes. We can deliver it to you. Very safe." He nodded again. "How it came into the country? I do not ask for details. If I had to guess, I would say, maybe through South America. Maybe Mexico. But that does not matter. We will send the sample to you. Then we will talk again."

One last nod. "*Do pobačennja.* Yes, goodbye."

He pulled the back off of the phone, removed the SIM card, and tossed it into an ashtray.

The sun came up over the lake, its reflection shining in the water like a golden egg.

Physics in Your Coffee Cup

"It wasn't your goddam fault, A.C.," Michael said, for about the tenth time. "Let it go."

The help had been sent home a little early, at ten-thirty. It had been particularly slow at the 1850 House, even slower than a typical week night. LaFleur usually tried to stay open until eleven to allow for the few late diners, the nine P.M. crowd, leaving them plenty of time for a leisurely dinner and with any luck, some expensive after dinner drinks. Tonight he and Michael had the place to themselves. And as a bonus, Michael wasn't on call for a change.

From behind the bar, looking as contented as a cat in a windowsill on a sunny day, LaFleur reached out for Michael's glass and poured him another generous shot of Famous Grouse. The bottle of scotch—an 18-year-old, from LaFleur's private stock—was being quickly depleted. "More ice?"

"Sure. Thanks."

As LaFleur leaned over and scooped a few cubes out of the ice machine, he muttered something under his breath.

"C'mon, A.C., I heard that, and no, I wasn't 'almost killed.' You were the one who just about bought the farm."

"Well, I'm damned glad we both got out of it in one piece. All it cost me is my boat, and you a few sleepless nights."

"Not something I'll ever look back on with fond memories," said Michael.

"Sure, but you know, it was not your fault either.

Nikki—well, how were you to know? She had everyone fooled. For years. Still, must have been traumatic."

Michael had been intimately involved—in more ways than one—with the arson case. He had started dating Nikki—a barmaid at a popular tavern—soon after LaFleur had agreed to help Maggie investigate the arson. LaFleur had been glad to see it. Michael was the classic tall, dark and handsome type, well-built and very athletic—tennis, swimming, golf—and had a touch of the exotic about him, having been born in the Dominican Republic. On top of it all, he drove a Mercedes sports car, an SLK350. Girls all over town swooned when he drove by. Even so, he'd not been in a relationship since a tragic incident several years earlier, an affair that had ended in a murder. LaFleur was the only one in Oswego who knew the story. And then, last year, Michael had become involved with the woman who he then discovered had been setting lethal fires around Oswego for years. She'd almost killed LaFleur. And if she'd been successful, she certainly would have gone after Michael next.

The experience had left Michael badly shaken—he'd taken a short sabbatical to decompress, and was only recently back at his anesthesiology practice at the hospital. This was the first time he and LaFleur had had a chance to talk since his return.

Michael hoisted his glass. "Never again."

"I'll drink to that," said LaFleur. He raised his glass and tipped it Michael's way. "Anyway, I can't afford to get involved in that kind of stuff anymore. This place is keeping me busier than a three-legged cat in a sandbox."

"Is that a complaint?"

"Just an observation," LaFleur said. "Wouldn't have it any other way."

"Speaking of cats, where is Newton?" asked Michael. Newton, a tabby that LaFleur had inherited from a less than conscientious vacation cabin renter a couple of years earlier, was usually holding court from a vantage point high on the back bar. He wasn't there tonight.

"Upstairs, asleep, waiting for Maggie," answered LaFleur. "Not enough going on down here. He got bored."

"He's forgiven you for nearly drowning him?"

"Hey, the damned boat was on fire, sinking," said LaFleur, waving his glass around. "It was like goddam 'Ice Station Zebra;' all that was missing was the polar ice pack. You know the story, right?"

Michael shook his head.

"Jaysus, don't you read? One of the best thrillers ever. Alistair McLean. There's a nuclear sub, under the pole, trapped under the ice. Pretty bad, right? Then people start getting killed, there's a spy on board or something; then, while they're trying to break through the ice, the sub almost floods, and they barely make it back to the surface. Can't get any worse."

LaFleur paused dramatically, raising his hands above his head. Michael waited expectantly.

"Then the goddam *engine room* catches on fire. On a nuclear submarine! Radioactive smoke, for Chrissake." He took a sip of scotch. "Well, that's about how I felt that night, getting off that damned boat, smoke and fire, Newton hanging around my neck as we crawled off onto the dock; don't know how we made it. Both should have drowned." LaFleur turned sideways, partially pulling his collar down on one side. "Here, look—I still have the scars where Newton latched onto me!"

"Yeah," laughed Michael, "I've seen them. So, has he forgiven you?"

"Hell, how do I know what that cat is thinking? But, yeah, he really seems to like it here. We all like it here."

"It's been a joy, watching you settle in here," said Michael, suddenly serious. "You belong here, A.C., you really do."

"Yeah, well. When old Joe died and the place closed

down, I never thought I'd be back in here again," said LaFleur. "And not on *this* side of the bar, for sure." He refilled his own glass, dropped a couple of ice cubes into it, and held it up to the light, slowly swirling the scotch. "I love the way the scotch and water create all those miniature currents around the ice as they start to mix. Sort of like the effect you get at the interface between a layer of salt water and fresh water, weird, distorted ripples and eddies. Fascinating physics going on there. Like the turbulence in your coffee cup when you pour in the cream. Fantastic. You get these beautiful effects, almost fractal, swirls within swirls, billowing clouds. Do it carefully enough and you can get what looks at first like a random mess that suddenly turns into beautiful concentric circles, before breaking back down into random clumps; thermodynamics in action. Entropy."

LaFleur paused, looking off into the distance, then back at Michael, who was looking a bit bemused.

"I never stir it up," LaFleur went on, "can't bear to destroy the effect. Hate to pick up the cup, take the first sip, mix it all up. Too many things mixed up as it is. Start mixing things up, can't tell what the hell's coming next. Worse yet, you can never un-mix them." He paused again, looking down at the bar as if looking for an answer to be written out there, a beer-stain codex.

"Oh, hell," said LaFleur. "What am I saying?" He tossed back a sip of Grouse. "Mix it up, damn it. Mix it all the bloody hell up."

Many Clickings

"This is no good," said Lev.

Val looked hurt. He had done exactly what Lev had asked.

Val's job as an orderly at Oswego Hospital had made it very simple; he had simply diverted some material from the radioactive waste bin at the hospital into one of the standard bins. Then Fedir had picked that bin up in a disposal van that had a couple of cheap magnetic signs on the door: "Lion Waste Disposal, Inc." No one had even noticed him coming and going. The van had been Lev's idea, and he was very proud of this subterfuge; he was even considering actually starting up a legitimate waste disposal business. He had learned that there was a lot of money in garbage in the United States. And it would give Fedir something to do during the day.

"Look at this," said Lev, holding out a bulky black box with crude symbols and Cyrillic labels stenciled in yellow paint, an old-style Russian military surplus Geiger counter. *Click.* Pause. *Click.* Lev shook his head. "This is not so good. We want *click-click-click-click-click*, many very fast clickings, yes?"

"This was what you said to get, whatever they have," Valentyn protested, "whatever is sitting out on the dock with a radiation symbol on it, you said."

"I know what I said. But this stuff, now I know it is no good. I looked up some things on the internet." He motioned toward the box, which contained a jumble of hospital waste—gloves, vials, cotton swabs, small utensils—materials typically contaminated in routine radiological tests. "What is in here is very low stuff, very short half life. I looked it up. It sits in the waste bin, in a few days or a few weeks, it is then not any longer radioactive, and it goes to the regular tip, the, what do they say here, the *dump*. Just regular trash. No one would look at this two times. I need something better. Something with more clicks."

"But we only need this stuff to be active for a few days," protested Val. "It should be good enough for what we're doing. And anyway, this is all they have."

"You are wrong there," said Lev, patiently. "You should know where in the hospital they keep the other materials, the ones with more clicks." He reached into his pocket and pulled out a slip of paper. "Here is a list. Figure out how to get this for me."

The reluctant look on Val's face began to annoy Lev, though his patience with his nephews was family legend.

"Your brother Fedir has already failed me in this, I will remind you, with his idea of smuggling waste from Nine Mile Point nuclear plant. Now he is stuck in a useless job, no access, no good to me.

"You will do this soon, yes?"

Val nodded.

"I know you will do a good job for me, Valentyn. You always do."

Talking Trash

"Val, are you here?" Karin called down the hall of Val's small apartment. Much too small, she was thinking; *how could I ever thought of living here?* Not to mention…well, her growing...misgivings? Mistrust? The way Val had been acting lately, distant and distracted; it made her wonder if something was going on.

"Val!" she hollered again, louder.

"What?" he yelled from the bedroom.

"Have you seen my hospital keycard? I can't find it."

"It was on the kitchen table last time I saw it," he called back.

He heard Karin rummaging around in the kitchen.

"I can't find it!"

Val came out to the kitchen, looked around quickly, and said again, "It was on the kitchen counter—"

"Well, it's not there now," Karin said, cutting him off. "I'm already late. And now I'll have to stop by Admin to get a replacement; that will take forever. As if I don't have enough to deal with. Damn it!"

"If you'd take more care—"

"Val, please." She walked quickly out to the living room and put on her coat; it was cooling off quickly in the evenings now. "Look around for it, will you? And call me at the hospital if you find it?"

"Sure."

"Okay, bye." She waited expectantly by the door for him to come over to kiss her goodbye as usual. He seemed preoccupied, and just stood in the kitchen, staring past her.

"Val. Bye."

He finally looked over at her. "Okay, yeah, bye, luv."

"Well, okay." She hesitated, then turned and went out, the door behind her closing with a dull thud.

Still standing the kitchen doorway, Val reached into his pocket, pulled out her keycard and held it up.

"Ah, here it is," he said, to the back of the door.

***

Karin hurried down to the apartment parking lot, distressed both by the inconvenience of misplacing her card and by Val's attitude. She got into the car and put the key into the ignition, but dropped her hand to her lap and sat there for a moment, eyes closed. Things weren't going well. Or maybe she was just imagining things. They had known each other for such a short time, she reminded herself. Maybe things had gotten too serious too quickly.

Karin had never gotten the whole story of how or why he and Fedir had come to America from Ukraine (not "*the* Ukraine," Val had taken pains to tell her). Apparently it had something to do with an uncle who lived a short distance away, near Pulaski, and the breakup of Val's family in Kiev. And conditions in Kiev after the dissolution of the USSR sounded grim. She was not entirely sure he was here legally. Little things Val let slip at times enforced this impression; but as her parents were immigrants themselves, her political beliefs on that topic were mixed at best.

In spite of what she perceived to have been an extremely difficult upbringing and an even more difficult transition to life in the U.S., Val was normally very amiable: lively and outgoing, quick to laugh. But occasionally, a dark current surfaced. Karin imagined it to be a cultural trait, an inherent gloominess she associated with Eastern Europe. But his Baltic mannerisms, his mysterious background, the accent, these were a big part of the attraction. The lure of the exotic. But Val's brother Fedir: that was a different story.

Karin was a little afraid of Fedir.

***

Once a week Val had to do a graveyard shift, with only eight hours off before starting his regular four-to-twelve. Hell on sleep patterns, but it provided an opportunity.

There were very few doors in the hospital controlled by electronic keycard. None of them were doors Val had authorization to open. Until now.

As the door to the radiological materials lab clicked open, he thought briefly of the trouble this could cause Karin. If the access record was ever checked, it would show her entering the lab—an area she normally had no reason to enter, and at a time when she was not even on duty.

No matter. If that ever happened, it would be much too late for anyone to make the connection.

He flipped on the light and pulled a note from his pocket, a list Lev had written out for him. Technetium-99. Radium. Gallium-67. Actinium-225. Iridium.

An hour later, Val pushed the cleaning trolley through a set of swinging double doors at a back of the hospital, into a waste holding area, muttering to himself in Ukrainian. It was a bad habit he'd been trying to break—whenever someone happened to catch him at it, it always led to suspicious looks. Just what he didn't need. He had enough to worry about without creating unnecessary trouble for himself. He'd worked hard, played by all the rules, made friends—everything he needed to do to establish himself in the community, even if at the lowly level of "maintenance technician," a demotion even by his standards. Life in Ukraine hadn't been so bad, he sometimes thought. But certain choices had been made, or made for him, and he had no regrets. None that he could afford. Lev was in many ways a wonderful uncle. In other ways…

He checked the door behind him to make sure it was latched before reaching down to the shelf at the bottom of the trolley to get a canvas bag. He set the bag down on the floor and zipped it open, and carefully removed a large lead-lined pouch, which he then placed in a small trash receptacle.

Since Freddy was also working that night, at the nuclear plant, he couldn't make the pickup the way he'd done before. It would have to be Jimmy.

***

The first few bars of AC/DC's "Back in Black" blasted tinnily out of the iPhone's tiny speaker. Jimmy glanced at the incoming ID as he answered.

"Yo. Vee-man. Wassup?"

Val understood none of this. "Jimmy?" he asked.

"Dude. What's the haps?"

There was some hesitation, then Val asked again, still puzzled, "Jimmy?"

"Yeah, man. This is Jimmy. Val?"

"Okay. Jimmy," Val said with relief. "What we talked about before, it's ready to go, okay? So, you can go there now?"

Jimmy nodded agreeably. "Sure, man, sure. On my way."

"Good, Jimmy. And Jimmy?" Val waited a moment until he was sure he had Jimmy's attention and there were no more incomprehensible Americanisms coming. "Jimmy, remember what I said. This thing you are picking up. Take it straight to the warehouse, to the building we talked about, yes? No stopping. No opening the bin. It could be dangerous, okay?" Jimmy answered in what Val had to assume was the affirmative. "The van is waiting for you at the place we said, yes?" he continued. "The key is on the floor, under the, under the thing, the floor thing. Okay?"

"Yeah, sure, under the floor mat, right."

"Straight to the drop off, Jimmy."

"*No problemo*, man. Like we said."

***

Jimmy drove around to the back of the hospital in the van he'd picked up in the deserted Price Chopper parking lot, a new Chevy Express Cargo. It had a sign attached to each side reading "Lion Waste Disposal, Inc." He'd spent fifteen minutes sitting in the lot trying to get his iPhone hooked up to the mp3 player but couldn't get it to work, so he just switched on the radio and tuned it to K-Rock. Val had had it tuned to WRVO, the public broadcasting station. There had been some kind of weird saxophone jazz playing when he'd started the van. He didn't want to listen to that crap.

There was no one around, as expected at this time of night. Val had said no one ever ventured out of the hospital late at night, other than coming and going through the emergency room entrance, the only entrance open after hours. Jimmy parked the van and turned down the radio before he got out, just in case. Didn't want to screw this up.

Val had said there would be a small red trash receptacle just outside the dock at the back entrance, off to one side.

The trash container was unexpectedly heavy—it was only about the size of a five gallon bucket—and Jimmy grunted as he picked it up and carried it to the van. He steadied the container on one hip as he pulled the keys out of his pocket and hit the side door button on the remote. The door rolled open smoothly.

"Cool," said Jimmy, placing the container on the floor. He glanced around the dock area, and seeing no one in sight, and no lights showing in the adjoining buildings,

Jimmy lifted the top off the container. He didn't see any reason to be left in the dark; after all, he was the one taking the risk here, not goddam Freddy.

The only thing in the container was a large, gray pouch. Jimmy reached in and pulled it out.

"Jeez, this thing's heavy," he grunted. He zipped it open and tilted it to one side, to get some more light. It looked like medical stuff; small boxes and vials of drugs or something. Then he noticed that some of the bottles and boxes were marked with a small yellow symbol. He reached in and picked one up to get a closer look. It was a radiation symbol. He put it back and looked at another one with a larger label; it read "Radioactive Materials," and next to the radiation symbol it was marked "GAMMA."

Shit.

Jimmy dropped the bottle back into the bag, zipped it up and put it back into the bin. Val had said this stuff was dangerous. Well, if it was dangerous, Val wasn't paying him enough. No, goddam it, Val hadn't said he was paying him at all, now that he thought of it. This was just supposed to be a favor. *Favor, my ass. We'll see about that.*

A few minutes later Jimmy was pulling up to the back door of an empty building on West 1st Street. As he stopped the van and looked around, someone opened the back door and leaned out a few inches, motioning Jimmy into the dark back room.

As Jimmy approached, he looked around nervously, like a cat just let out of its carrier at the vet.

Then he recognized Bullet Head, who was holding the door open for him. "Is Lev here?" Jimmy asked, as the door closed behind them. Bullet Head motioned by tilting his head to one side. "There." Jimmy had never heard him utter more than one word at a time. He turned as Lev came walking out of a dark room at the front of the building. Jimmy followed his gaze.

"Hello, Jimmy. Thank you for coming." Lev stood there, expectantly, as Jimmy just stared.

"Jimmy!" Lev said. "The bin, Jimmy. Do you have the bin?"

"It's in the van."

Lev's shoulders slumped as he said in exasperation, "Go get it!"

A minute later, Jimmy returned with the trash bin. Bullet Head took it from him and carried it into a front room, as Lev followed. "Wait here," Lev said, waving Jimmy back.

Jimmy stood there quietly in the dim light, straining eyes and ears, trying to get a clue. He could hear muffled noises from the other room, along with parts of a low conversation between Lev and Bullet Head, before they came back out to where he had been waiting.

Lev was brief. "That is all we need from you now, Jimmy. You can go."

Honorary Maple Leaf Fan

The Bondurenko brothers left Oswego at three-thirty A.M., Fedir driving. It was a cold wet night, a dank, Kiev October kind of night. A drizzling mist hung everywhere.

It was over four hours to Toronto, so they figured they'd get there around eight-thirty in the morning, and get to a PATH parking garage and into the underground by nine. That would leave two hours to do their scouting. They planned to leave by eleven, and be back to Oswego by three-thirty or so.

Val studied the PATH map he'd downloaded to his iPAD, reading off impressive statistics to Fedir.

"Twenty-eight kilometers of shopping mall. One hundred thousand daily commuters!" He looked over at Fedir. "One hundred thousand!"

"*Odna tisjacha?*"

"No, stupid, you must practice your English. Not 'one thousand," one *hundred* thousand."

Fedir glanced at him, uncomprehending.

"*Vī zrozumilī shcho iā skazav?*" Val asked. "One hundred times one thousand. Do you understand?"

"I understand," said Fedir, belligerently. "My English good as yours."

"'You say, '*is as*' good."

"*Shcho?*" What?

"Forget it."

The rest of the conversation transpired in Ukrainian, the only English being Valentyn's continuing reports on details from the PATH brochure. "World's largest underground shopping complex." "More than fifty office buildings connected to PATH." They were most interested in the Stock Exchange and TD Bank. He was also not sure exactly where the Canadian Stock Exchange building was, and didn't see it on the PATH map, but had seen a picture on Google Maps. He was sure it was close by and they could find it.

"Ah, look here, on this map, Union Subway Station, very close to Toronto-Dominion Center." Fedir looked over, craning his neck to study the subway map Valentyn was holding out.

"*Khristos*, watch the road, Fedir," Valentyn said, pulling the brochure back.

They parked on Wellington Street, a long walk in order to see what they wanted to see, but they were good walkers.

In the next two hours they visited several underground shopping areas, but did not buy anything, stopped at four transit stops, Valentyn making notes, and had a gelato. Once back above ground, they wandered around the general area for awhile, mistaking the old Toronto Stock Exchange building for the current one before finally locating the right building—the stock ticker running around the outside of the building had been a good clue—and went to the Pravda Vodka bar on Wellington Street hoping for some much-needed sustenance, but it didn't open until four P.M. As they prepared to leave for home, Valentyn bought a Maple Leafs T-shirt at a kiosk not far from the car park.

"Hockey," said Fedir. "Is bool-*sheet*."

"Shut up, Fedir. It makes me look Canadian. We're buying you one next time."

***

When they got back to the house, Lev was out on the back deck overlooking the pool. Lake Ontario glittered a couple of hundred yards beyond; waves slapped the beach with a rhythmic beat.

"This lake," Lev said, looking out across the water as they approached, "it is much like our *chorne more*, our beautiful Black Sea. Do you boys remember the beach house there, the house at Zatoka?"

"Of course, near Odessa," said Valentyn. "We were all there with you and Shashen'ka when we were very young."

"Yes. Yes, that is so. Your *titka*, your aunt, Shashen'ka, yes? She loved that house very much. Very much." He took a deep breath. "She would have liked this house, this lake. I think so."

Lev stared out into the night, across the Black Sea. Val and Fedir stood silently behind him, afraid to move or sit. They had seen him in this mood before. "He took it all from us. Everything we all worked for so many years," Lev said.

"Mendelokov," Val said, softly.

"*Tak*, yes, Mendelokov," said Lev bitterly. "That bastard Mendelokov, that, that—" Voice rising in pitch, he sputtered to a stop, speechless in his fury, his disdain. "It is not for me that I do these things. You know this. It is for Shashen'ka. For my brother. For your parents. For you."

"Yes, *dyad'ko*, we know," said Valentyn.

Lev looked up at Valentyn and Fedir, remembering. Their father, Lev's brother Petro, had been a doctor in Kiev, and had treated Shashen'ka before she died of an inoperable liver cancer. Lev had been a successful broker and financial advisor, though perhaps a bit more successful than could be easily explained by his day-to-day business dealings. Soon after Shashen'ka's death, both Lev and Petro had been financially ruined in a massive energy stock fraud perpetrated by a Ukrainian mobster named Sergei Mendelokov. Lev blamed himself for Petro's losses, as he had been the one to bring him into the scheme. Petro, already a bit unstable, and now unable to cope with the financial catastrophe that had suddenly devastated their family, had committed suicide. Val and Fedir's mother had died two years later. That is when Lev brought them to America and began to plan his revenge. Not only revenge, he told himself, but nothing less than the restoration of his family and fortune. And he would do anything to attain that goal.

"So, boys, now, we get back what is owed to us. We get it back. And maybe more, yes?" Lev stood, stretching, groaning at the effort of rising from his low patio chair. "We have all we need for the job in Toronto. You know exactly what you will do there, yes? You saw no problems at the, what do you call it, the PATH?" Val assured him that they were ready to go. "Good," Lev continued. "But—what we do in Toronto is only part of our job. It is very important, as we just talked. But," he repeated. "You know we have another job to do also. And for this we need the jeweler."

Lev led Valentyn and Fedir back into the house, to tell them what they had to do now.

Cold Hands, Warm Heart?

About one in the morning, LaFleur was awakened by a noise downstairs. His first impulse was to grab the Glock from the bedside table—the gun that no longer resided there, as a concession to both his retirement and to Maggie, now that he was no longer taking on unofficial murder cases. The pistol was now on a shelf in the closet, available if needed, but not so available as to be too easy. Loaded, of course.

After he heard the door close and the lock turn, a moment's reflection reminded him why he no longer kept a weapon quite so handy. It was just Maggie, coming in from her volunteer shift at the Crouse burn center in Syracuse. Normally she'd have been at the 1850 House with him, acting as LaFleur's hostess, but once a week she did a stint at the hospital, and LaFleur had to act the part of host himself. He preferred running the bar, but schmoozing out front as customers came in was good PR.

Fifteen minutes later he was about to fall back to sleep, Maggie spooning against his back. They fit together nicely—both about the same height and weight, both still slim and fit, although Maggie's dark red hair did not have as much gray in it as LaFleur's.

"Cold stomach," he mumbled.

"I left my jacket unzipped on the way over from the parking lot. Just for you."

"Ummm. Cold stomach, warm heart, is that how it goes?" LaFleur said.

Maggie snuggled a little closer.

"You're not really that sleepy, are you?"

"Can't sleep, anyway," he answered, and then turned his head in the sudden realization of how that might have sounded. "Not that I'm not interested—"

Maggie laughed.

"Michael was here earlier," LaFleur went on, "and we were talking about the fire, you know, and how things turned out. He's feeling a lot better. Hope he can forget about it. Guy needs a break in that department."

"Yes, he does."

They lay there quietly for a minute or two. Then LaFleur turned, turning Maggie over onto her other shoulder, and snuggled up closely behind her.

"Ummm, cold butt, warm heart?" he asked.

"You never get that right, do you?"

"Right enough," LaFleur said. "Right enough."

"Do you ever miss it?"

It took a moment for him to switch gears.

"Ah. The force? Not at all."

"But whenever a case comes up…"

"Which has been exactly twice since I retired. Both at your insistence, if I recall correctly. And as I've said before, never again."

"I think you *do* miss it. And in spite of the, well, complications, let's say, of the two cases you've taken on since you retired—"

"Complications?!"

"Okay, more than complications, I'll give you that. But still, you enjoyed it. Both times, I could tell. Maybe the challenge of it; the sense of accomplishment."

"Maybe."

"And the chance to make a difference."

"Some difference. Nothing ever really came of either case, I botched them both. No real—well, anyway," he finished, lamely.

"You weren't about to use the 'J' word, were you?"

"Maybe."

"If anybody has a right to, you do."

"Hmm. 'Cold justice, warm heart?' Is that how it goes?"

"You're incorrigible."

"I try."

An Incident

"Karin!"

Pulling her hands out from under the scrub room sink faucet, Karin turned and looked back over her shoulder. It was Marla, the head nurse.

"What?" Karin called out.

"There are some policemen here to see you."

Karin turned back to the sink and continued scrubbing. "I'm busy." *Why were early morning shifts always so hectic around here?*

"Karin?" Marla repeated, more urgently this time. "Did you hear me? Police. They want to talk to you."

"Can you ask them what they want?" Water ran off her elbows as she held her arms up at right angles.

"I did. They wouldn't say."

"Jeez. Dr. Uva will be here any minute; we've got, uh, Mary? Marilyn? Anyway, a Caesarean scheduled in, what, twenty-five minutes. Tell them I'll call them back later or something."

"Okay."

Marla was back less than a minute later. "They say they have to talk to you now."

"Marla, I just can't—"

"They said it's important."

With a resigned sigh, Karin slapped the faucets shut with her elbow, shook her hands partially dry and grabbed some paper towels. "Tell them I'll be there in a minute, but I don't have much time."

She watched Marla nod and back out of the door. She

finished drying her hands, and then walked out to the floor station still in scrubs and surgical cap, mask hanging at her neck.

A tall man in an ill-fitting blue suit and a uniformed officer were waiting at the nurse's station. Karin, still peeved, walked up and said, a little shortly, "I'm Karin Broussard. What do you want?"

"Hello, Ms. Broussard" the suit said politely. "I'm Detective DeSalvo." Motioning to the officer beside him, a skinny kid with a buzz cut holding his hat in front of him. DeSalvo went on, "and this is Officer Spence. Is there somewhere we can talk?"

Karin looked around distractedly. "Um, well, yeah, we can use the surgical waiting room. No, wait; there might already be a family in there." She looked down the hall. "I think there's an empty room. This way."

Once in the room, she turned and looked at them. She restrained from putting her hands on her hips, though that's how she felt.

"Ms. Broussard, your—" began the young officer.

"Mark, please," interrupted DeSalvo.

Spence's face turned red as he stammered, "Sorry," and looked at his shoes. *Must be a rookie*, Karin thought. She looked back at DeSalvo, eyebrows raised, *well*?

"Ms. Broussard, there's been an…incident…at your father's jewelry store. Late last night—"

"What do you mean, an incident? I haven't heard anything from him, he would have called. What—"

"Ms. Broussard, please." Karin suddenly felt reprimanded, just like the kid had been a minute ago. She took a breath to calm herself.

"Sorry, please go on."

"Late last night there was apparently a break-in at your father's business. It was reported—"

Karin could not help herself. "Apparently? And it 'was reported?' Did you respond to an alarm? I would have heard from him by now if something was wrong."

"I'm sorry. 'Apparently' was not the right word. There was a break-in. But it was not discovered until this early morning." He held up his hand to stop another interruption. "We responded to the premises after a call from a delivery person." He glanced at Spence, "UPS?" Spence nodded.

"But my father, is he okay? What happened? Why didn't he call?"

"We believe the break-in occurred at about one A.M. this morning," DeSalvo continued. "There was an…altercation."

Karin felt her stomach tighten as she unconsciously backed away from DeSalvo a step or two, until she was stopped by the edge of the hospital bed. She absently reached up and removed the scrub cab, letting her hair fall half into her eyes.

"Ms. Broussard, I'm afraid there is no easy way to say this."

Suddenly, she knew. Sweeping her hair up out of her face with both hands and looking up into DeSalvo's eyes, she knew. She had seen doctors do this, many times. A failed surgery; a terminal diagnosis; an unforeseen complication. She knew. And, looking into his eyes, she could see that DeSalvo knew that she knew.

"I'm sorry," DeSalvo said.

Want a Grilled Cheese Sandwich?

"Val!" Karin hollered into the dim hallway, the apartment door closing behind her. There was no answer.

She'd come to Val's apartment straight from the hospital; another nurse had been called in to cover for her.

She closed the door behind and slumped against it, closing her eyes against the dead weight of no answer. *He should be here; his shift doesn't start for hours.*

She heard a noise in the kitchen, Val clumsily banging a drawer closed, or banging a pot lid, or dropping something into the sink for her to clean up later. As usual. Something smelled bad.

She walked through the small living/dining area into the even smaller kitchen, feet almost dragging with the dread of what she had to say. Val looked up as she came through the doorway. "You look like hell," he said.

Jesus, help me. I don't need this.

"What?" Val said, seeing the look on her face. In her eyes.

She looked around the kitchen distractedly and saw a burned grilled cheese sandwich on a paper towel next to the sink. *For breakfast? Well, he keeps odd hours. Maybe he's going to throw it away later. Or maybe he's still going to eat it; he doesn't seem to mind those kinds of things.* "I've eaten worse," he often said, after ruining something.

Karin made an effort to concentrate. "Val, there's something...something's happened."

Val stared at her, uncomprehendingly, expectantly, impatiently; she wasn't sure how to read his face. *Well?* he seemed to be saying.

She turned suddenly and went back out into the living room. She sat down on the couch and called to him. "Can you come out here?" She heard the water run in the sink for a moment, and then Val came out, drying his hands on a dish towel.

"What is it?" he said, somewhat more sympathetically, sitting down next to her.

"It's…it's my father."

He sat silently at her side.

She turned her face to him, trying to get him to look at her. He continued to look straight ahead. She turned back to stare in the same direction, staring at nothing. "He's been killed," she said.

Val put his hand on her shoulder, clumsily, and then dropped it to his side. "I'm sorry," he said.

Her shoulders sagged and she almost turned to him, almost reached out to hold him. Almost. He remained still.

They sat there without speaking.

That's it? Karin thought. *Just, "I'm sorry?" No, "what happened?" No, "Oh my God, how terrible?"*

"I've got to go," she finally said.

***

She felt lost, drifting; like that time she was twelve and had gone out too far on the lake in the canoe. It seemed to take forever to drive the ten minutes back to her apartment.

She almost made it into the bedroom before she broke down and cried.

Jimmy Helps Out

Karin unlocked the door to Armand's Fine Jewelry ("We Buy Gold," it said a small sign in the window), and stepped into the shop, locking the door behind her. She crossed quickly to the alarm panel and disarmed the system. In the sudden silence, the shrill noise of the delay signal still echoing, it hit her—the shop should have been open hours ago. Armand standing behind a display case cleaning the glass; peering through a loupe at someone's now unwanted diamond ring; gazing out the front window. Wondering how life had become so…unfulfilled, so unsatisfying. So lonely. Karin had seen it coming on for months, a distant, searching look whenever she came in the door and found him there alone.

She took a deep breath and made her way up to the apartment. She felt as if she had a thousand things to do and nowhere to start.

Jimmy was supposed to meet her here—she glanced at her watch—in about two hours. She had spoken to Jimmy only briefly since the murder. It had all been so chaotic. She could hardly bear to think about it. In any case, she knew he would be no help whatever.

She forced herself to go into the bedroom and looked around. Neat as a pin. Book closed, dust jacket flap marking his place, on the night stand. The covers were pulled back carefully on the corner of the bed just as he'd left them when he'd gotten up to go downstairs. Even if Armand had become a bit flighty in recent months, a bit lost, he certainly hadn't become any less fastidious.

She tossed her purse on the end of the bed and started going through dresser drawers. Pushing the reality of what she was doing into a small space in the back of her mind.

***

About three hours later she heard pounding at the back door. *Must be Jimmy, finally.*

She went down and through the back of the shop, momentarily disoriented by the clutter—papers scattered, tools lying scattered on the benches, a chair pushed into a corner, out of place. Thankfully, no obvious evidence of the actual murder remained; the police had been nothing if not quick and efficient, and had already had a service in to do that bit of unpleasantness. They'd finished all too quickly, she thought—how could they have gotten everything they needed so fast? Didn't forensics take longer than that? She'd had the feeling they were just going through the motions, but she had convinced herself later that it was just shock. She'd hardly been able to speak to them that night. Not that it had been all that much better when she'd tried to follow up. More hollow assurances, everything possible was being done, these things take time—*then why did you rush it so much*, she'd felt like saying. We'll call you as soon as, etc., and she'd finally had enough and broken down, just so they'd stop all the dithering.

Jimmy pounded again. Why hadn't he come to the front?

"Okay!" She pulled open the door and Jimmy came in.

"Sorry I'm late," he said. No explanation. She didn't ask for one.

"I've been upstairs, trying to sort out some of the personal stuff. See if there's anything that might—" She waved her hands. "Help," she finished.

"Yeah, I'll help," Jimmy said, trying to sound sincere and indignant at the same time.

"No, I mean, I thought maybe I would find something that might help, you know, find the—help find out what happened."

"Oh, yeah, sure," he said.

They stood staring awkwardly at one another for a moment.

"You haven't been around much," she said, keeping her voice as neutral as possible. She knew how unreasonably defensive Jimmy could get.

"Yeah. Well…"

"Okay. Never mind. Um, now that you're here, and we happen to be in the shop, you want to start down here? The police say they're finished already."

"Did CSI:Oswego come up with anything yet?"

"You haven't talked to them?"

"No. I was going to stop at the station after I left here. Thought maybe something had turned up."

"No." She rubbed her eyes. "Let's just get through this the best we can, okay?"

"Sure."

She looked around, a weary look on her face. "This is a mess. Where do we start? Did he keep his papers in here somewhere?" she asked, moving to a filing cabinet sitting next to the desk.

Jimmy shrugged. "How would I know?"

Karin threw up her hands in exasperation. "Well, if you'd ever taken the trouble—"

"Damn it, just let it go, will you? This was never right for me, you know that."

"Nothing ever was," Karin replied bitterly. She looked around the room again. "All right, forget it. Let's just get this done." She motioned to Jimmy to come closer. "Isn't there something missing here?" she asked, pointing to the side of the desk. "When you talked to the police, did they ask you if anything was missing? I was so upset that I don't remember them even asking, but I must have talked to them about it." She looked up. "That safe, or box, whatever, he used it for the scrap gold, that old thing he lugged around all the time. Shouldn't that be here? I thought this was where he usually had it sitting."

"I guess so; I don't know." Jimmy looked around. "It's right over there," he said, pointing under a table off to the side.

"Okay, yeah," Karin said, leaning down and peering at it. "That looks like it."

"So, you haven't looked at his records yet?" Jimmy asked.

"Some. What do you mean, exactly?"

"Did he have anything scheduled? He usually went to Canada, every month, without fail. Do you know when he was going next?"

"Jeez, Jimmy, how the hell do I know? There are papers scattered all over the place. Anyway, it can't be that important, can it? We'll figure it out later."

"Well, I just thought, you know, if there is something that needs to be done, well, I could do that. Make the delivery, I mean. Be better to get all that out of the way, wouldn't it? Get all the pending business cleared up as soon as we can?"

Karin looked at him as if he had just dropped in from Mars. "What the hell do you care? You made it clear a long time ago that you didn't want to have anything to do with it. Now suddenly, you're interested in the business?"

Jimmy didn't respond.

"Am I right?" Karin demanded.

"That was before, well, before this happened. I just thought I could help get things straightened out. And, well, Lev has something—"

"I'll let you know," Karin said, cutting him off, barely registering what he was talking about. *I don't need this, not now*. It was becoming a litany.

She repeated her earlier question. "So, again, when you

talked to the police, what did you tell them, did they ask if you saw anything missing?"

"I told them I didn't know if anything was missing or not."

Karin decided she might as well drop it; Jimmy wasn't being very helpful. Then she remembered something else. "Oh, and another thing," she said. "I *think* I set the alarm when I locked up after the police left. It was set when I came in today. But I'm not sure; did you set it?"

"No."

"And they said it hadn't been set at the time of the break in. Doesn't that seem strange to you?"

"Yeah, I guess so, but maybe he was just getting forgetful, you know? Old people do that."

"No, he was always very careful about setting it. Do you think there could have been a problem with it? Why would he—?"

"God damn it, Karin. I don't know anything! I don't fucking know!"

Jimmy threw the back door open and stalked out. The breeze from the door slamming behind him blew a pile of papers off of the desk onto the floor at Karin's feet. She stood there staring down at them for a long time before stooping to gather them up, but when she finally had them in her hands, she couldn't really see them anymore.

Never Again, Again

LaFleur was in the back going over inventory with his restaurant manager, Big Frank, when the phone rang. It was Michael, calling from the hospital.

"Hi, Michael. No, I'm not too busy," he said in reply to Michael's query. "What's up? Nothing wrong, I hope?"

"No, nothing wrong, exactly," Michael hedged.

"Well, what is it? I'm old, you know, and can't stand too much suspense."

"I'm afraid you're not going to like it, A.C.," Michael said.

"Wouldn't be the first time you've been the bearer of bad news. Though I keep hoping you'll change your habits."

Michael paused. "We've got a new case for you," he finally said.

Silence.

"You've got to be kidding."

***

The next morning, LaFleur found himself sitting at the table in Doctor's Corner pouring a second cup of coffee for Maggie, Michael, and Karin Broussard.

Karin was slim and petit, dark haired, quiet and demure, yet radiating the quiet confidence of a senior nurse. Maggie had spoken highly of her while they were waiting for her to arrive.

While LaFleur filled her cup, Karin explained that she

had contacted Michael immediately after her father had been killed because she felt the police were giving her the runaround, and because she knew of Michael's involvement in the investigation into Angie Frascati's death. She'd hoped Michael could help; she had known him for several years—they had been on the verge of a real relationship at one point—and she trusted him. Michael had in turn talked to Maggie, whom he felt had more leverage with A.C. than he had, and she had quickly arranged the meeting.

LaFleur sat looking down at the table, absently scratching the back of his neck, a gesture Maggie recognized as reluctant interest, even though he had told Maggie earlier that he saw no chance of this going anywhere. The problem wasn't that it was still officially an active police case—he'd been around long enough to know that didn't mean much, from either side of the fence. It had just been too short a time since the loss of his houseboat, and all that had gone along with that. He'd finally found a comfortable place for himself—his reopening of the 1850 House had been welcomed by the whole town—and he was reveling in the newfound feeling of usefulness, and enjoying the extended camaraderie that was quickly growing up around the venture.

"Okay," LaFleur said as he looked up at Karin, "even though, as I just said, I probably can't get involved, for a lot of reasons—" He interrupted himself with a rather theatrical sigh. "Tell me again why you think I can do anything about it? Now, don't misunderstand me," he hurriedly qualified, glancing at Maggie as her eyes began to narrow, "I'm just trying to determine why you think the police aren't capable of handling this. You said a minute ago that you had a meeting with Chief Boyko; let's go back to that. What did he tell you?"

"Nothing." Frowning.

"Well, 'nothing' is not much to go on..." He let that

hang, prompting. While he waited, he pulled a small notebook and a pen out of an inside sport coat pocket. He still dressed like a detective rather than a restauranteur; Maggie was trying to replace his wardrobe but it was slow going.

Karin sighed now, heavily; LaFleur thought she might be mocking his performance of a moment ago, but on second thought decided it had been genuine enough. And he'd promised Maggie he'd reserve judgment, he quickly reminded himself.

"Maybe I'm rushing it," Karin admitted, "but it's just that he seemed more interested in making the whole thing go away than actually doing a real investigation. He said the shop had already been examined very carefully before I got there—by his 'crack forensics team,' he called them—and that nothing in the way of evidence had been found. No fingerprints, no weapons, nothing. And he seemed very reluctant to talk about what steps would be taken from this point. So I guess I am not really giving them a chance, but I want to do everything I can, as quickly as I can, to find out what happened. That's why I called Michael so soon."

"Okay, I can understand that," said LaFleur. "Let's talk about some possibilities. How about a burglary motive? Any evidence that the placed was being hit, and your father just happened to interrupt it? Was there anything missing?"

"We're not sure. I'm trying to sort it out now. I know there was nothing taken from any of the cases in the shop—no jewelry, watches, nothing; the cases looked like they weren't even touched. And there was jewelry sitting on the workbench in back, too. There were a lot of papers scattered around, and an open filing cabinet, but other than that—well, I just don't know at this point."

"Okay, fair enough. Um, you said 'we're not sure.' You and—?"

"My brother Jimmy. He came over to the store while the police were there, but he didn't stay long. He's never had much to do with the business; he and my father never really got along. It's been even worse, lately."

"How can I get in touch with Jimmy, does he live here in Oswego?"

"Yeah, he's renting an old a place over on East 6th. I'll give you the address. I don't think he has a phone, not at the house, but his cell number is still good." She shook her head. "Doesn't have two nickels to rub together, but somehow he manages to have an iPhone. With an unlimited data plan." LaFleur handed her the notebook and pen; she wrote down Jimmy's address and phone number and pushed them back across the table to LaFleur.

"Any work number?" he asked, glancing at the notebook.

"Jimmy?" Karin laughed. "No, no work number."

"You said your father hadn't planned to be home that night, I believe," LaFleur continued.

"That's right," Karin answered. "He went up to Toronto that afternoon. He has one client there that he deals with on an occasional basis, oh, two or three times a year, maybe. Almost all of his gold business was with Earl Dufresne. In Kingston. The police say he's their prime suspect, but that's ridiculous. I know Earl. He's harmless. He always had a good relationship with Dad. I think the police just picked out the easiest person they could find that had a connection."

"Well, the dealer in Toronto. Any reason to suspect him?"

"I can't imagine why. Like I said, it was only a couple of times a year. It wasn't all that profitable to go all that way, or convenient. Dad always made a little outing of it, since it's several hours away, and it was hard for him to get away during the day. He'd usually arrange an evening meeting, then stay over and drive home the next morning. Mom always complained. Anyway, he came home early for some reason."

"No idea why?"

"Not at the moment. I've got a call into the jeweler up there, but he hasn't called back."

"Name, number?"

"I'll get that for you. I don't have it with me. I think his name is Antoine. But I can't remember his last name at the moment. Something French-Canadian. Of course."

"Why 'of course?'" LaFleur asked.

"Oh, I guess I just meant that Dad was very old fashioned. He had a lot of connections, but it always seemed that his real friends in the business were all French-Canadian. Old ties die hard."

"And the police, here, they've talked with this guy?"

"Yeah, but police say they don't know anything more about it either. They say they've contacted his regular clients and have been questioning them; I gave them what I had the night of the—" She broke off. "But nothing's come of it. Not yet."

They all sat there quietly for a moment. LaFleur sipped his coffee. "I hesitate to ask," he said, "since I might be able to get the information from the police report, but maybe you have more…um, immediate…information. Can you tell me the cause of death? And again, I'm sorry, but did they tell you what…uh, what…" He broke off uncertainly. He had never had this kind of trouble questioning anyone, witnesses or victims. He was used to a more formal setting, certainly, but it really shouldn't be this hard. *I really shouldn't let myself get involved in these things.*

Karin rescued him from a more prolonged interrogation. "It was a blow to the head, they said."

"Did they recover—?" *Damn it.* "Did they recover a murder weapon?"

"No. They just said it was something solid, heavy, maybe cylindrical."

"Thick, thin, big, small? More like a bat, or like a—"

He stopped himself as Karin began to shrink back into her chair, eyes widening a bit. "Jesus, I'm sorry, I didn't mean to…I can get everything else I need from the police," he finished lamely.

Another heavy silence ensued. Uncomfortable glances were exchanged. Maggie glared. Michael pointedly studied his coffee cup. Karin looked out the window.

Maggie finally broke the silence. "And you said no alarm, Karin? No call to 9-1-1?" she asked. LaFleur nodded at the question gratefully, pleased at the reminder; he'd meant to ask that first thing.

"No," Karin replied quickly. "That's what's so odd about it. He is always very careful about setting the alarm, every night. He was very jumpy, especially since our mother died. He's never lived alone before, and was having kind of a hard time of it, I think. I tried to be there for him…well, I am there as often as I can be, but—"

She stopped and picked up her coffee cup. Her hands were trembling slightly. It was at that moment, as LaFleur heard her speaking of her father in a confused mix of past and present that he suddenly decided to take the case.

I Hear Canada is Beautiful This Time of Year

It was very late.

Jimmy barely heard the phone, and it took him a while to find it in the clutter he called his living room.

"Hello, Jimmy?"

"What? Who is this?"

"Jimmy!" Val shouted. "Turn down the music!"

Jimmy reached over and turned down the volume on the low-budget iPod docking station, which had been blasting the dulcet tones of Twisted Sister at full volume through three-inch speakers.

"Go."

"Jimmy, we need your help again."

"What is it?"

"Just meet me at Lev's in thirty minutes."

***

Jimmy was shown into the library by the dark suit he'd been calling Bullet Head. He'd recently learned from Val that he was Lev's bodyguard and right-hand man, named Vasily, and was not to be trifled with. Jimmy had no intention of crossing him; he looked like he could take someone's head off with one swipe of his large right hand.

Coming through the library door, Jimmy caught a snippet of the conversation that had been taking place before his arrival. It was in English, which surprised him—the Bondurenkos typically spoke Ukrainian among themselves—but when he entered he saw it was because Lev was on the phone. Just like the other night; it sounded almost like the conversation he'd heard then.

Lev waved him back out the room with a glare. Jimmy bumped into the door, causing it to bang against the door frame, eliciting another, more intense, glare from Lev. Vasily pulled Jimmy out of the way and carefully closed the door, nodding with a frowning apology to Lev.

Jimmy's encounter with Lev during his recent delivery to the abandoned building had made him more than curious. What he'd just heard in the library confirmed his belief that there was a lot more to this than Val had been telling him. But he hadn't had a chance to think much about it, given everything else that was going on. Suddenly he was ushered back into the library by Vasily.

Lev showed no signs of his previous annoyance and welcomed Jimmy in his usual, expansive manner.

"Jimmy, Jimmy, come in, come in. Please," he said pleasantly, motioning to a chair next to where Val was sitting, "please sit. *Bitajemo*, again, to my home." Lev raised his hand to Val. "Valentyn, get Jimmy something to drink."

Val went about pouring a shot of vodka at a sideboard behind Lev's desk. He carried it over to Jimmy, who barely glanced at Val as he took it from his hand, simply murmuring a quick "Thanks, man."

"We have another job for you, Jimmy," Lev said. "A simple delivery, scrap gold."

Jimmy sipped at his vodka. This didn't seem like one of those times to throw it back in one shot. "Um, this isn't really a good time, Lev."

Lev glanced at Val, glared a long moment at Fedir, and then turned back to Jimmy.

"Ah, yes. I am sorry, Jimmy." Lev just sat and looked at him, as if lost in thought. Jimmy sat there uncomfortably, not sure where this was going and not knowing what to say.

Lev finally spoke again.

"I would understand if you cannot do this for me now, Jimmy, but it is very important. We have made some arrangements that, well, would be very difficult to change. If I could make it a later time, of course I would, but it is just not possible." He lowered his head slightly, and then looked back up at Jimmy imploringly. "I know I am asking a lot, Jimmy."

Jimmy took another sip of vodka, then tipped the glass back and drained it. He held it up to Val. Val refilled it and handed it back. "What is it you need, Lev," Jimmy said, looking down at the floor.

"This thing we want you to do," Lev continued quietly, "is very simple, but requires someone with the right skills. The right, well, we should say, 'the right stuff,' yes?" Lev beamed. "That is the saying, yes, *right stuff*? From your cosmonauts, I mean, *astronauts*." Lev beamed even brighter, proud at knowing this Americanism. "Well," Lev then amended, toning it down a bit, "I mean, you will have the right stuff after we get you all fixed up. If you agree," he quickly added.

Jimmy looked up and nodded warily. *WTF*? he thought, but more prudently asked, "What do you mean?"

Lev motioned to Val. "Explain, please."

Val shifted forward in his chair and leaned toward Jimmy "Yeah, Jimmy. We have something special for you to deliver to Canada for us, like we said before, you remember? And we don't want to have any customs problems. Lot of trouble, and maybe some of the things we are sending, they might not think it is just scrap, you know, and make us pay customs duty, fill out forms, all that; or maybe they won't let us take it in at all. We don't know. And we are foreign; they don't like that."

Jimmy knew what it was like to be discriminated against. Of course, in his case, it was self-inflicted. He had not made himself popular around town in the past year or so. "Well, yeah, I guess if that's the case, I can talk to Karin, see what I can do." Jimmy sipped at his vodka. "But even if Karin goes along with this, there is still a problem."

"What problem?" Lev and Val asked in unison.

"I don't have a FAST pass," Jimmy answered. "That was my father's—"

Another uncomfortable silence engulfed the room.

"We have a pass for you," Val said, quickly. "It was very easy." Actually, Val had been up all night working on it. He reached into a leather pouch sitting near his feet and pulled out a folder. "Here, see. It is ready to go," he said, handing a small card to Jimmy.

"Wow," was all Jimmy could muster at the moment, though he still said it with some admiration.

"You can see that the photo is not exactly what you look like now," said Lev, pointing.

"Oh, yeah," Jimmy replied, looking more closely at the card. The photo—*where did they get the photo, anyway*? Oh, at the party, they were taking pictures. That had seemed odd. But the photo had been slightly touched up. "What's with the short hair?"

"You will be crossing the border, carrying certain items that will be classified as commercial, um, commerce items, sale items. Scrap gold, just like what your father did, as usual," said Val. "So you need to look more, um, normal, you know? More like a businessman. So, tomorrow, a haircut, a new suit. You'll look great. You'll do it?"

"Well, I guess so," Jimmy said. "But are you sure this is okay? It will work, get me through? Don't they check against a database or something? Immigration, man, they're tough. I don't know." Jimmy was looking for an edge, something he could use as leverage, something he could use to get out of this. They seemed too desperate, he thought, too pushy.

Lev glanced at Val before answering. "It is taken care of; your pass will work just fine. You do not need to worry." He extended his arms to Jimmy. "You do this favor for us, yes?"

"Well, yeah, I guess so," repeated Jimmy, still reluctantly.

"Well, then," said Val. "It's all set. You can go to Kingston early in the morning." He paused. "You'll be back in Oswego by noon."

Jimmy looked around, sensing that the meeting was over, but wondering if maybe there was time for one more shot of vodka. Before he could hint at that, Lev leaned forward.

"There is something else," Lev said. "You remember the delivery you made to me?"

"Yeah, sure," Jimmy answered.

"We want you to take that along with you also."

"Okay." He sat there quietly, waiting for more.

"That is all, Jimmy."

"Oh. Okay, then." He stood up and slowly left the room.

He had really wanted that third shot of vodka.

***

On the way out, Jimmy managed to take Val to the side and quietly ask him to come out to the car with him, without getting Lev's attention. Vasily had already gone back to wherever it was that he stayed when not doing Lev's bidding, like a robot returning to its charging station.

Jimmy leaned on the hood of his car, arms folded. Val stood by silently, waiting.

Jimmy hadn't thought this through that well, but figured he had nothing to lose. It was obvious that they needed his help. But it was just as he suspected—they were taking advantage of him. He had even heard Lev say it again, *favor*.

"I'll tell you right out, Val," Jimmy began, "I want to

know what the deal is. And," he said, putting up his hand to stop Val's reply, "and, I want in on it. It looks like there's some heavy shit going down"—Jimmy had always wanted to say that—"and I'm not going to risk my balls for nothing. What's going on?"

"Jimmy, Jimmy," Val said. "We'll bring you in when it is time. We just can't—"

"No, goddammit. Now. I want to know what the hell is going on. That shit I delivered to Lev, it was radioactive, right?"

"Did you look in the case, Jimmy?" asked Val.

"No, hell, no," Jimmy lied instantly. "I mean, yes, I just glanced in it. Just for a second, and I saw a radiation symbol on something. I'm not stupid, Val. And I heard Lev on the phone with someone. He was talking about Toronto, and this radioactive shit, and I want to know what's going on. And now you say there might be 'other items.' What, I'm supposed to just do this, without knowing what I'm doing? No way. I want in, Val. I want a cut, there's obviously money in this, like, why are you smuggling stuff into Canada? What?" Jimmy had started waving his arms around.

"Okay, Jimmy, calm down. I guess we were asking too much, too soon. We should not ask you to do this thing for us for nothing. You are right." Jimmy was nodding in agreement while Val spoke, but still waiting for something specific, something solid.

"So? What makes any of this worth my while?" Jimmy asked. "This is a *very* bad time, Val."

Val looked around as if gathering his thoughts. "Okay, Jimmy. I will tell you the truth," he said. "In Ukraine, our father, Lev's brother, Petro, he is a doctor in Kiev. And you know I work at the hospital in Oswego, right?" Jimmy nodded, wondering where this was leading. "So, in Ukraine, the hospital sometimes has trouble getting some things, some more difficult things; expensive things. The case you delivered to Lev, it did contain radioactive materials, things used in medical tests and treatments, cancer treatments. My aunt Shashen'ka, Jimmy, she died of cancer because some of the things she needed were not available. Some of the medical tests, the radiation treatments, could not be given to her in time; the hospital did not have what they needed. Shortages like this are common in Ukraine. So, Lev, he wants to make sure this does not happen to other people, like it happened with Shashen'ka."

Val paused. Some of what he had just told Jimmy was true to a point—Shashen'ka had died of cancer, but not due to hospital shortages, and their father had been a doctor before his death. But that really had nothing to do with they were asking Jimmy to do for them. But a story was beginning to come together, a story he believed Jimmy would fall for.

"So," Val continued, "we get some small amounts of the radioactive materials, very low in radioactivity, from the hospital—where they have a lot of this stuff, more than they need—and we send them to the hospital in Kiev. There is very little money in this—yes, we sell it on the black market, but through a friend. Not for the money, but for the hospital." He looked at Jimmy closely. "You see, Jimmy? What you took to Lev; that will first go to Canada, and then it goes to the hospital in Kiev. We cannot send it from the U.S., the customs watch too closely, and we have not the right contacts. We have some people in Canada who can get it to Ukraine. That is why we need your help."

Shit. "So, no money?"

"Well, Lev doesn't have to know this," Val said, looking over at the house as if Lev could hear them, "but I think we can get you something, to make it worth your while, as you say."

"You're not shitting me?"

"No, Jimmy. We will take care of you."

"Okay, well, then I guess I can do it. If it's that important."

"It is very important, Jimmy. I will give you more details when we are ready for you to take the shipment, okay?"

"Okay. Sure, Val."

"Goodnight, Jimmy. I will call you."

***

Val stood and watched as Jimmy backed his car out of Lev's driveway and drove off. He gave a small wave, then turned and went back into the house, muttering under his breath in Ukrainian—which roughly translated would have been something like *stupid bastard*. When he got back to the house, Lev was waiting.

"Well?"

"Yeah, he'll do it. This will be even better than before, you know?" Val was the one who had originally convinced Lev to use a courier; a "mule," he'd said, to transport the materials across the border.

Lev had never been completely comfortable with this plan, but also had to avoid any problems related to getting the various materials into Canada. Had Val and Fedir been caught smuggling radioactive material, everything would have been put into jeopardy: the stock deal, the financing, and the final delivery of the contraband to Semilovich all depended on safe transport. Using locals, with no visa or passport complications, and especially using Broussard, with the jewelry connection, that had seemed like a very good option. Circumstances dictated that it all had to happen in Canada, not the United States, which would have simplified things. But taking advantage of Mendelokov's current weakness to cash in on the stock market, and the sale of the material to Semilovich had to happen in Canada, and Lev was not about to pass up the chance. And now Val was obviously anxious to clear himself with Lev, after the new problem they'd just had. The problem Fedir had created. Fedir was so uncontrollable.

"Yes, maybe so," said Lev, after a few moments. "But, nothing can go wrong this time. This is all getting too complicated."

"No, Lev, listen," Val countered. "It's really much simpler. We can have Jimmy take the thing directly to Pavlo, in Kingston. No messing about with the other guy, that Dufresne. That was always going to be tricky. And we can get the other stuff up there the same way, still using Broussard's customs passes. Much easier than what we were going to try to do."

Lev seemed to brighten somewhat at that, if reluctantly. "Yes, okay," he finally said. "Then it is all right, Valentyn. Your friend Jimmy, he will make this good after all."

They're Just Not Biting Today

The downtown police station hadn't changed much since he'd retired, LaFleur noticed as he walked through the main entrance and back to the administrative area. There was the same tarnished coffee urn sitting on a chipped and stained Formica table, dispensing dishwater thinly disguised as coffee, miniature plastic cups of milk-like substance piled in an old bowl to serve as whitener, a dilapidated box full of pink and blue sweetener packets next to it; he'd always had to bring in his own cream and sugar. Today he politely turned down the offer made by the sergeant as he was escorted through to the chief's office.

Chief of Police Matthias "Matt" Boyko—"Boyo" to those who knew him well, not a particularly large group—barely glanced up as LaFleur was ushered into the room, the sergeant belatedly nodding permission for him to enter before closing the door quietly after him. LaFleur took the seat not offered, crossed his legs, and sat back. He'd seen this type of behavior too many times to be either impressed or intimidated by it, and knew Boyko well enough to see through the bluster. They'd actually had a pretty good working relationship at one time, LaFleur mused. He was sorry, but not too surprised, to see what Boyko'd come to. Some can handle authority, some can't. LaFleur had never wanted to be a bureaucrat, and had sidestepped the chance more than once. Boyko'd lived for the opportunity and had progressed through the ranks quickly; the petty power grabs, back-biting, and tawdry maneuvering had come to him easily. LaFleur didn't trust him as far as the edge of his oversized desk.

When Boyko finally deigned, after several minutes, to acknowledge LaFleur's presence, it was with an immediate dismissal.

"Sorry, LaFleur; can't help you with this one."

This was not unanticipated, based on LaFleur's earlier conversation with the lead detective on the case, who had been equally uncooperative, almost to the point of rudeness. He'd given LaFleur a copy of the police report, but refused to offer any more information, or allow access to the post mortem. It was the attitude more than the actual refusal that LaFleur had found most disappointing, even given the general deterioration in the force that he'd seen since he'd left.

"Not like I'm asking for much," LaFleur started to say, "I have a copy of the preliminary report—"

"Who gave that to you?" Boyko asked sharply.

"Your precinct captain. Just a few minutes ago."

Boyko glared, obviously unhappy to hear this. "Shouldn't have. Open goddam case. No discipline…" He appeared to LaFleur to be close to muttering as his voice lowered, then stopped talking and sat silently, still glaring.

"Well," continued LaFleur, "if I could just get whatever you have on this other jeweler, Dufresne—" Boyko cut him off.

"That's good, not wanting much, LaFleur, because that's what you're getting, not much. Not much at all. Diddley-squat, as a matter of fact. We can't have every Tom, Dick, and Harry"—Boyko loved talking in clichés—"coming around here sticking their noses into our business, interfering with ongoing investigations, and especially not you, LaFleur," he went on, pointing emphatically, "given your recent, 'blowup,' shall we say? It's a good thing I wasn't in charge during your little escapade; things would have been done much differently, I can tell you."

LaFleur restrained himself admirably and ignored the

gauntlet, simply replying with raised eyebrows. When it was apparent that Boyko was done with his rant, LaFleur started to his feet. "Well, yes, Boyo"—he watched Boyko cringe—"I imagine you would have done things differently, if you'd even been aware that something was going on, that is. That's the problem around here lately. Lack of interest, I'd call it." LaFleur was reaching for the door handle. "So, if you're not interested in what I've learned from Broussard's daughter, I won't force you to listen." He opened the door. For a short moment he was afraid that Boyko hadn't taken the bait.

"What do you know, LaFleur?"

"Do I get some cooperation in return?"

"No. This isn't 'Let's Make a Deal.' If you know something, you're obligated to turn it over."

"Well, in that case, I guess I don't know anything after all." He went out the door.

"LaFleur—" Boyko half raised himself out of his chair, glowering.

"Write if you get work," LaFleur called out over his shoulder as he continued down the hall.

Sometimes they took the bait. But then again, sometimes they took it and just spit it out.

That Old Trick?

She set her purse down on the floor as she came in, dragging her coat off at the same time, and flopped down on the couch.

What a horrible week.

She was "dog-food tired;" she almost smiled at the thought. It was one of her father's favorite family jokes. When she was small, four or five, she had tried to imitate something she had heard him say once after coming in late for dinner one night, that he was "dog-tired." From that day on, whenever anyone in the family expressed fatigue, they were dog-food tired.

Apparently Val and Fedir had not heard her come in; they were not expecting her. She heard them talking in the kitchen; well, she could really only hear Fedir's voice clearly. He had a belligerent tone, and his voice was coarser and deeper than Val's. He sounded like an ignorant peasant, she thought, before guiltily repressing it. And they were speaking Ukrainian, so it didn't matter.

She sat there, drifting. Fedir's voice was even harsher in Ukrainian than in English, she thought. Val's voice was a soft murmur in comparison. Occasionally his voice rose in pitch slightly, as if trying to get Fedir to agree to something, or understand something. Fedir was none too bright.

The voices grew louder, and Karin realized they were interspersing Ukrainian with English, sporadically, Val confidently, Fedir hesitantly, Val repeating things in what sounded like an attempt to get him to understand, sometimes switching entirely to English.

"No, no, Fedir, 'short' does *not* mean 'not tall' in this way, it is a technical stock trading word. We sell stock we do not have, at a high price. Then when it is quickly very cheap, we buy what we need, and then when the price is high again—a short time later—we sell it. We make a lot of money. *Rozumiyesh?* Understand?"

She could almost hear the implied "stupid" in Val's demanding "understand?" Fedir replied in Ukrainian.

"Damn it, Fedir. It is simple," Val continued in English, probably just to annoy Fedir, she thought. She listened as he explained short selling again, in even simpler terms. Fedir seemed to get it this time, and they went on, but in Ukrainian again.

But as they went on, Karin began hearing English words, like "Canada" and "crash," along with Russian or Ukrainian names, but used with the English word "boss." Other words sounded a lot like their English versions, with Val sometimes also using the English word. She heard something in Ukrainian which she quickly realized was "radioactive" or "radioactivity." A few seconds later, Val used the word again, followed by *irydiy, strontsiy,* and *radiy,* and the English word "radium."

What the hell?

They continued talking, now about Toronto; they seemed to be interested in something in the PATH underground. Banks? Rail stations? None of it made much sense.

She stood, carefully slipped on her coat and picked up her purse. *Okay, so it's an old trick. It's worked before, with Dad.*

She quietly opened the front door, and then quickly slammed it closed.

"Anyone home?" she called.

73

Jimmy Crack Corn

The house on East 6th needed paint; this area had never really recovered after Diamond Match shut down. LaFleur didn't like thinking about how long that had been. Early fifties, he thought.

A screen door had detached itself from the front door frame and lay crookedly against the house, blocking the doorbell. LaFleur knocked loudly, in order to be heard over the heavy metal music echoing through the peeling clapboard siding and grimy windows. Knocked again, even harder, after no response. The music suddenly stopped, and a few seconds later the door opened.

"Yo, what?" said Jimmy, blinking in the sunlight. He looked stoned. About what LaFleur had expected, a skinny long-haired creep; Karin had prepared him for the worst. Still, LaFleur was determined to give him the benefit of the doubt, for now. But before he could respond to Jimmy's inarticulate "hello," Jimmy made another attempt at communication.

"Uh, sorry, can I help you?" Jimmy amended, realizing that: one, he didn't know who was standing on the porch; and two, it might be someone important. Either that, or some semblance of manners had taken root somewhere during his upbringing.

"My name is LaFleur. I'd like to talk with you about your father's murder." Sometimes a direct approach was called for. Jimmy blinked again, but no invitation in was forthcoming. "Your sister Karin asked me to look into it for her," LaFleur continued. "For both of you." He wasn't sure he was getting through; perhaps by showing some sympathy?

"Oh, yeah. She told me. Sorry, come in, come in," he said, holding the door open wider. LaFleur stepped into the front room as Jimmy closed the door behind him.

"Uh, I'd ask you to sit, but, well..." Jimmy said, motioning around the nearly empty living room with outstretched arms. A single beanbag chair sat like an island in the middle of the room, a small end table holding an iPod docking station next to it. LaFleur hadn't seen a beanbag chair in ages. Various items—glasses, bottles, a couple of dishes, some candy wrappers—had washed up around the chair, the flotsam of a dissolute life.

"Won't take long," LaFleur said shortly. *Hope not, anyway.*

Jimmy stood expectantly by the beanbag.

"I'll try not to ask you to repeat what you've already told the police," LaFleur said. "You talked to them last, when?"

"Uh, yesterday. They wanted to know if I knew the jeweler in Kingston, Dufresne."

"Do you?"

"Not very well. They seemed to think I should. He's a suspect, right?"

"As I understand it, yes."

"So, you haven't found out anything about, um, his involvement, or more about the, the...about his death? My father's death," he clarified needlessly. Jimmy, in spite of his estrangement from Armand, was having a hard time expressing the reality of what had happened. LaFleur had never gotten used to this part of it; no matter how close or distant a victim's family had been—and according to Karin, Jimmy and Armand had been anything but close for quite some time—murder changed everything. As many times as he'd seen it, it was still hard to watch.

"Well," LaFleur said, "I'm planning to talk to Dufresne

right away, since I was told he is, or was, a suspect. Other than that, no, I don't know much of anything that the police don't know. Yet. I was hoping that you…?" He left the query open, not wanting to push Jimmy in any particular direction. *Not that this kid doesn't need some direction.* Which Jimmy then proceeded to prove by just standing there, staring blankly at LaFleur. *Oh, well.*

"You were close to your father?" LaFleur asked, prodding.

"Uh, we had our moments."

"You weren't involved in the business, though, according to Karin. In spite of his wishes?"

"Yeah, I guess. He used to think I'd take over or something. Not my thing." Jimmy shifted from one foot to another, like a small kid embarrassed by adult conversation.

"But still, you knew something about the business, right? Even helped out occasionally in the past, and, again according to Karin, kept the option open?"

"He was a hard man to say no to."

LaFleur nodded, and then changed tacks.

"One thing the police wouldn't talk to me about"—an allowable fib, in this circumstance, since they had practically refused to talk to him at all—"was the state of the murder scene"—Jimmy didn't flinch this time—"in terms of a motive of burglary. Do you know of anything significant missing from the shop, anything he may have kept particularly secure? Anything unusual? Any special items, anything someone may have known about that would have prompted something like this?"

"Jeez, I don't know. I don't think so. As far as I know, there wasn't anything missing, not even any slag."

"Slag? Isn't that something left over from a blast furnace?"

"Scrap gold. His name for it. Old rings, cheap gold chains. Dental crowns, even. Stuff people brought in looking for a quick buck. It wasn't the main business, that's for sure; that was always the real jewelry. But there was some money in it."

"That's the Canada connection then, the scrap gold, the *slag*?"

"Yeah. He had a whole thing worked out using customs preapprovals and things, he had a special track. Pretty slick, actually."

LaFleur's eyebrows went up. "Your sister Karin called me a little while ago and told me she thinks there are documents missing from your father's office," he said. "Travel documents, special customs passes, IDs. That the kind of thing you're talking about?"

"Yeah," he said. "I guess."

"She hasn't talked to you about it?"

"No."

"And you don't know of anything else missing, anything out of place?"

"Don't think so."

LaFleur reached up and ran his hands through his hair in frustration, an old habit he'd tried to break for more years than he could remember. "What's going to happen to the business?" he asked.

"Guess Karin will take over."

"But she has a full time job; she's a nurse, right?"

"Well, yeah. So, I don't know."

"Has she asked you to help out, figure out what needs to be done next?"

"There are some things that need to be taken care of, I guess; Karin's going through the accounts now. I don't know. Maybe."

Maybe what? Jimmy hadn't finished his thought.

"Anybody else know much about his dealings in Canada?" LaFleur continued. "Besides Dufresne, that is. Anyone local involved in the gold trade?"

"I don't know."

LaFleur could see that this was going to go nowhere;

he'd dealt with a thousand Jimmys in his day, and was in no mood to continue the charade. He could always come back to him later if necessary. He turned to go, saying that was all for now, but then—and as he did this he couldn't help but think of the old Columbo TV show—he turned back and said, "Just one more thing, if you don't mind."

Jimmy nodded. "Sure."

"Karin's boyfriend, um, Val…" LaFleur pulled a small notebook from an inside pocket of his sport coat—he was the only person he knew without an iPhone—and flipped a page or two, mostly for effect, even though he knew this kind of police theatrics no longer impressed anyone. "Yeah, uh, *Valentyn Bondurenko*," he said, pronouncing the name carefully. "Karin is involved with him, is that right? Know anything about him?"

Jimmy shuffled his feet as he answered. "No. Um, well, no, not really. Well, some. Just a little."

"Oh." Not exactly what LaFleur had heard. Not only from Karin, but other "sources" that LaFleur cultivated around town. Jimmy was in deep with Bondurenko. Why was he hiding it? He scratched a reminder into his notebook to follow up. Also with Karin. "Well, I guess that's all, for now, anyway. Can I contact you later if I need to; let's see, at this number?" He read Jimmy's cell number from the notebook.

"Uh, sure. Anytime." Jimmy grinned and swept his arm out grandly toward the door. "Can I show you out?"

LaFleur looked around the room once more, for the first time seeing something likeable in the kid, and laughed.

"No, I think I can make it. Thanks."

All Dressed Up & Somewhere to Go

Karin tried Jimmy's number again. She'd been trying to get in touch with him for hours. His phone wasn't even taking messages; he'd either not bothered to set up his voice mail, or forgotten, or didn't care. It was all the same to Jimmy.

Miracle of miracles, he answered.

"Yo."

"Jimmy, finally. I need to see you again. Can you come over to the apartment?"

"Your apartment?"

"No, sorry. Dad's. There are some insurance papers, and you also need to sign some papers for the bank. I'm there now, can you come over?"

"I'm kind of in the middle of something. How soon do I have to be there?"

"I'll be here awhile. When can you come?"

"How about an hour?"

Karin repressed a sigh. "Okay, fine. See you in an hour." *Probably be two.*

***

When she opened the door, after an hour, almost to the minute, she couldn't believe it; it took a few seconds for her to realize that it was Jimmy standing there. Short hair, clean-shaven, wearing a new suit. A tie. *My God. A miracle.*

"Jimmy!"

"Well. Yeah. I told you I'd come over."

"Yeah, but, well, look at you! What, did you get a job or something? Or do you have an interview, I mean, or, well…" She flapped her hands in confusion for a moment, and then seemed to have a revelation. "Oh," she said. "Oh, Jimmy. This is for the funeral, isn't it?"

Jimmy managed to look embarrassed, tugging at an earlobe and shifting his gaze away from her eyes, focusing somewhere in the apartment behind her. He was still standing outside the door.

"Uh, yeah. I thought, well—"

"Oh, Jimmy," Karin said, "Thank you." She stepped forward and put her arms around him, laying her head on his shoulder.

Jimmy awkwardly tried to reciprocate, reaching back and patting Karin on the back a couple of times, even while carefully backing up to disengage.

"Uh, Karin, it's not what you…uh, it's not anything to get all worked up about." She dropped her arms and stood back.

"Well, I appreciate it."

Jimmy hung his head for a second, almost tried to tell her again, but then realized he'd be better off to just go with the flow. That's what he was best at. "Anyway, what do you need, you said some papers or something?"

Karin turned and motioned him to come in, talking as she walked to her father's desk. "I've been trying to figure out what the burglary was all about. Nothing in the shop was touched. Nothing in the back room was touched either, other than the desk and a filing cabinet. There was still a pile of old jewelry sitting on the bench. There were papers scattered around the room—well, you saw it, right?—but it just doesn't make sense to me.

"Anyway, that's not why I called. I have death certificates, they need to go the bank and to the insurance company; you need to sign these two documents." She didn't bother trying to explain in any detail.

Jimmy, as expected, didn't question her. He signed and said, "That all?"

"Sure, sure, that's all for now."

"Well, what about making a delivery?" Jimmy suddenly asked. "You just said you found a bunch of gold sitting on the workbench; it's probably supposed to go to Dufresne, right? I can do that tomorrow."

Karin blanched. "*Tomorrow*? Why tomorrow? Can't we just wait and—"

"I want to get it done, get it out of the way. I thought you'd welcome the help," he added.

She shook her head in frustration. "I've been thinking about this delivery thing ever since you mentioned it. For one thing, I don't even know if you can get through customs. For another, there are some papers and things that seem to—"

Jimmy cut her off again. "Just let me do this and be done with it, will you? I can handle it. I have all the documents I need."

"You do? When did this happen?"

"I've always had them," Jimmy lied. "When I was working with Dad."

Karin could only shake her head again, this time in resignation. *I don't need this*, she thought for about the hundredth time. "Yeah, take it. Whatever." Her least favorite phrase, '*whatever*.' She heard it from Jimmy all the time. Now he had her doing it. *So much for the new Jimmy.*

Whatever.

A Weighty Discovery

Karin let LaFleur in at the back door. After a brief "hello," they both stood there quietly for a moment, LaFleur gauging Karin's mood, and Karin looking around nervously, as if she expected to have to act as a guide. LaFleur was thinking about how uncommon it was for a close relative to be involved like this, so soon after a murder. But since Boyko appeared to have shut the investigation down practically before it started—where had he seen that before?—the burden had fallen on Karin. He intended to make this as easy as possible for her.

"Thanks for meeting me here on short notice. I know you must be, well, pretty overwhelmed right now. Please don't feel you have to hang out in here while I take a look around. If I have any questions…"

"Oh, no. Please, I'd like to stay. I want to help."

"Okay, that's fine. I appreciate it. Shouldn't take long. Maybe I can find something the police missed."

"Considering how much time they spent here, I don't doubt it," Karin said bitterly.

"Yeah, well. Not what you expected of Oswego's finest?"

"I'll withhold judgment. But so far, no, not happy."

"I'll do my best to make up for it. I've got my reputation to uphold." He smiled, glad to see Karin return it.

"Where do we start?" she asked.

"Let me just look around a bit."

Karin held out her arms in a sweeping gesture. "Kind of

a mess. I haven't done much in here, just poked around a little. Most of the insurance papers and everything else I need right away I found in a fireproof box in a closet upstairs."

LaFleur looked back over his shoulder as he walked around the small room. "Thought about what you're going to do with the business yet?"

"No, I haven't started thinking about the day-to-day stuff yet. Dad always thought Jimmy would sort of take it over someday, but nothing ever came of that. They barely talked for, oh, the last year, at least. They hardly ever saw one another. I think I told you; Jimmy was never that interested in the business. Though he's not interested in much of anything these days." She paused. "Oh, and I asked him about the alarm, if he thought there could have been a problem with it or something. Whether it was on or off when the police left; I think I reset it, but it was all so confusing. But he didn't want to talk about it." LaFleur made a quick note as Karin continued. "And it was strange, too, when he was just here? He asked if he could do a delivery; take the latest collection of scrap gold to Canada."

"Is it urgent?"

"No, not at all. I don't understand why the sudden—" She looked over at LaFleur with a frown, scratching her head. "I think he said something about Lev. That doesn't make sense, though. Does it?"

"Lev?"

"Val's uncle. Lives out in Pulaski somewhere. Jimmy has been doing some work for them or something. He hasn't said much about it. But I'm sure Jimmy mentioned Lev when he asked about the scrap shipment." She shrugged. "Well, I'll deal with that later. Sorry."

"No, might be important. Anything about the business."

"Okay, I'll ask Jimmy about it again. He's going to Kingston tomorrow."

"Huh." It was LaFleur's turn to scratch his head.

"Tomorrow? I have to agree, that is sort of, well, unusual, given the circumstances."

"Maybe I misunderstood. We didn't have a very good meeting. But I'll ask him about it tonight, if I can."

"Okay. Now, you say you don't see anything missing? Nothing out of place?"

"I can't say for sure. I didn't come back here very often, not lately."

LaFleur walked back over to Karin, and pointed at a rack of scale weights sitting on a table next to the desk. The scale—an old brass balance type—was on the table next to the weights. The weights were made of cylindrical brass, ranging from very small to rather large. "I noticed something when I came in," he said. "There's a weight missing, on the right end. One of the big ones." He moved closer. "See here? Goes from one kilogram to the largest, three. The weight in between is missing."

Karin leaned toward the weights LaFleur was looking at. "Yeah, I see. The two kilogram weight?"

"Must be." He looked back at the weights for a moment, and then turned to Karin. "What did you say the police told you about the possible murder weapon?"

"Something small, solid. Heavy."

LaFleur held out his hand, fingers curled as if holding the missing weight.

"About that size?" he asked.

Who Do You Trust?

Val came out of the house to meet Jimmy as he drove up, carrying a large zippered bag and a metal strong box. Val opened the van door and put both items on the floor behind the driver's seat, next to Jimmy's safe, the one Armand always used.

"The bag contains the medical items we talked about, okay? The one you took to Lev. It's very important; you just leave the bag with the person at this address." He gave Jimmy a slip of paper with an address, nothing else. "The box contains the scrap gold we want you to deliver," he said. "But before you deliver it along with your other gold, you must also take it in with you; this person will look at it before you take to the jeweler."

"Why?" asked Jimmy.

"Don't ask questions, Jimmy. He just has to look at it, that's all. Then you take the box and make your delivery. And don't mess around with it, okay?"

"Sure, Val, okay."

As soon as he got out of sight of the house, Jimmy pulled the van over at a wide spot in the road and stopped. He twisted in his seat, then reached back and picked up Val's box and set it on his lap. He flipped up the lid.

It looked like the normal crap he'd seen before, when he had still been working with his father. A bunch of cheap gold chains, a few bracelets. Some old brooches, regular yard sale stuff. He poked a little deeper into the box, pawing around and shoving stuff aside. Suddenly, like a magpie spying a shiny object in the grass, he noticed a large golden locket, about three inches tall and two inches wide, and an inch think. It had an unusual cross inscribed on the front panel, like a regular cross, but with a short crossbar at the top, above the main cross, and another short slanted bar at a forty-five degree angle across the lower portion of the cross. It looked foreign. Some sort of Russian Orthodox thing, he figured.

He picked it up to have closer look, holding it on his palm. He couldn't immediately see how it opened. Holding it there, peering closely, looking for a seam or a latch, it took a minute for it to hit him.

The locket was warm.

Unusually warm.

He dropped the locket with a start, piled some jewelry back on top of it, then slammed the lid on the box and put it back on the floor behind the seat. He started driving.

Every once in a while he raised his hand and glanced at his palm.

What the fuck?

***

The address in Kingston Val had given him was for a crappy apartment downtown. The guy—no names were exchanged—could hardly speak English (*no surprise*).

The Russian—*Ukrainian,* Jimmy reminded himself—was stoned out of his mind; Jimmy had no trouble recognizing the condition. *Bet Lev wouldn't like that.*

Jimmy put the bag and strong box down on the floor. Pointing at the bag, he said, "So, that stuff goes to a hospital in Kiev, huh?"

"Hospital?" the guy said. "No hospital. What hospital? No." He laughed.

Jimmy pressed him, angling for more information. "The stuff in the satchel, it's medical stuff, for a hospital in Kiev.

Lev's brother or something. They said that stuff is very hard to get in the Ukraine."

"I don't know what you are saying." He bent down and picked the bag up, opened it quickly and glanced inside, then zipped it shut and dropped it back onto the floor. "What a sweet deal," he said.

What deal? Jimmy thought. *What is Val not telling me?* He decided to try to lead the guy on. "Yeah, it will be nice. Hope they can pull it off." He paused after getting no reaction to "pull it off." That had probably made no sense to the guy, Jimmy realized. "When are they going to make the deal?" he asked instead.

"Soon," the guy said. "Soon." Then he picked up the strong box and carried it into the next room. Jimmy listened through the open door as the guy dumped the contents onto a table and sorted through it. Then he noticed he could see the guy in a mirror on the opposite wall. *Stupid bastard doesn't know I can see around the corner.*

The Ukrainian was pulling jewelry out in handfuls onto the table, not paying too much attention to it. Then Jimmy saw him pick out the big golden locket, the one with the strange cross on it.

The guy looked nervous. Lev hadn't acted that way with the hospital stuff. Jimmy watched, becoming more and more suspicious, as the Ukrainian pried it open with a small screwdriver, took a quick look inside, then closed it and dropped it into another small box and set it aside. Then he scooped all the other jewelry back into the strong box and brought it back out to Jimmy.

"Good. You go now," he said.

***

The delivery of the gold to Dufresne had been a pain in the ass; the jeweler had been questioned about Armand's murder just two days before, after all, and was still pretty jumpy about it. In fact, he'd told Jimmy he was expecting a visit from a detective assigned to the case later that morning—Detective LaFrance? Something like that. Jimmy'd said, yeah, don't worry, he's a good guy, not bothering to correct him on LaFleur's name.

Dufresne had kept Jimmy for over an hour, alternately expressing his sympathy, relating old stories about Armand, and complaining about the treatment he'd been given by the American police. He'd said he hoped this LaFrance guy was different. Jimmy had assured him that the detective was working for Karin and not to worry.

Jimmy had been anxious to get away, and had finally just abruptly said "goodbye, been nice to see you again," and left. He'd been afraid Val would think something had gone wrong; Val had told Jimmy to call him as soon as everything was finished, and it was getting late. Fortunately, Val hadn't sounded concerned when Jimmy finally called, and appeared to be pleased with the price Jimmy'd gotten for the gold; Jimmy thought it was a little low.

He could hardly keep his eyes on the road. *Goddam Bondurenkos. Lying bastards. Who do they think they are? Goddam Lev. Slimy bastard.*

How do I get myself into these things?

Jimmy glanced in the rearview mirror, suddenly paranoid as he approached the Canada/U.S. border. The trip on the way up had been uneventful; the border agent had taken the customs pass, scanned it, then handed it back, no questions asked. He'd quickly glanced into the safe, as Jimmy opened it for him, but didn't ask to see anything else. "Have a nice visit, um, Arm—um, Mr. Broussard," was all he'd said, distractedly waving Jimmy on.

The border crossing came into sight as Jimmy rounded a slight curve. He slowed, stopped, and handed the agent his FAST pass. No problem; he cruised right through.

Val had some explaining to do.

Duty Free

Cash-for-gold, at least in Canada, LaFleur had heard, was a real circus.

The jewelry business, a normally conservative, even staid occupation conventionally, had become enveloped in what many in Toronto called "gold frenzy." By 2009, with gold at a thousand dollars an ounce and no end in sight, dealers began to engage in protracted television and newspaper ad wars, featuring outlandish characters and ever more hyperbolic come-ons. There were sidewalk altercations between jewelry dealers who had worked across the street from one another, amicably, for years. The most outrageous behavior became commonplace. What had started as an apparently harmless but heated rivalry between two of the biggest dealers in Toronto had turned into an ugly confrontation involving fire-bombs and an alleged plot to hire a hit man—woman, actually—to take out the competition.

The dealer the Oswego Police Department had targeted as their one and only suspect did not operate out of Toronto, but Kingston, where gold frenzy had not taken on the fever pitch of Toronto. Armand Broussard had done the majority of his dealings with this jeweler in Kingston, Earl Dufresne. A quick internet search by LaFleur's young friend and IT consultant, Raymond "Blueray" Levine, had turned up nothing unusual in Dufresne's business. The jeweler had often styled himself as "Goldbug Dufresne" in his advertisements, but by Toronto standards he was eminently boring. LaFleur had scheduled a meeting with

Dufresne for that afternoon. Dufresne had been polite but guarded on the phone. This was going to turn into another wild goose chase, he could feel it.

As LaFleur drove across the bridge onto Wellesley Island, he rehearsed what he'd learned from the police about Dufresne, which wasn't much. No convictions, no financial problems, no history at all, really. Though the investigation had been cursory at best, in LaFleur's opinion. Someone had talked with the Canadian authorities about the murder, but hadn't had much cooperation beyond an agreement to look into the case in the future should the need arise. The RCMP had not been all that interested in talking with some flunky in a small town force, LaFleur suspected. Reciprocity was fine on paper but in practice it seldom worked out that well; too many CYAs on both sides always mucked up the works. But then again, he told himself, I can be a cynical bastard. Oh, well. Maybe he could learn something. You never knew.

Pulling into a passenger vehicle lane at the Thousand Islands Bridge border crossing, LaFleur pulled out his passport. He'd long ago stopped using his police credentials, unlike a couple of retired cops he knew—they just couldn't let go of the badge-flashing habit; LaFleur didn't need the ego boost.

"Business in Canada, sir?" the agent asked as LaFleur slowed to a stop.

"No commercial business, if that's what you mean," said LaFleur. "On sort of an errand for a friend."

The agent looked quickly into the empty back seat of the classic Pontiac Grand Am, then turned to LaFleur and smiled. "Have a nice visit, eh?" he said, waving LaFleur through.

As LaFleur drove slowly away from the checkpoint, he noticed a van coming the other way with a large magnetic sign on the side displaying a modernistic lion's head logo, and below that, "Lion Waste Disposal, Inc. Oswego, New

York." He'd been having trouble with the local disposal company, but hadn't known of an alternative. He'd have to look them up when he got back. Maybe they were a small outfit just starting up and there could be some savings there. Everything added up in this business, he was quickly finding out. Even the amount of ketchup he put in the little dish along with the French fries. He'd noticed that most customers were leaving about half of the ketchup in the dish; using smaller containers would save at least fifty dollars a month, he figured, probably more.

As he accelerated away from the border crossing, he noticed the Duty Free shop on the other side of the highway and remembered he was almost out of Dr. McGillicuddy's Peach Schnapps at the bar. He stocked it especially for one customer, the owner of the Oswego Comic Shop, Arlene. For some reason LaFleur had so far been unable to determine, it was the one variety of McGillicutty's schnapps that was not imported into the U.S, and the only brand Arlene would allow him to use in her specialty drink, the one featured on the new 1850 House drink menu—Arlene's Zombie. It had been invented in honor of one of the best sellers at the shop, which for quite some time now had been anything related to "The Walking Dead." Instead of the usual apricot brandy, Arlene's version used peach schnapps, but only Dr. McGillicuddy's would do. The description on the menu was a small commercial for Arlene's—she'd practically saved his life last year, after all—"any customer who can drink two of Arlene's Zombies and still walk gets a voucher for a free The Walking Dead comic book at The Comic Shop." The small print stipulated "no more than two per customer, or you may really become one of the walking dead."

But Arlene's part in saving his life was another story, one LaFleur had recently tired of telling, "if the truth be known," a favorite expression of his father's, which LaFleur had learned even before he knew what it meant, and which he sometimes felt was a near impossibility. He did not really expect to get the "truth" from Dufresne. His motto on the force had been "Everybody lies, all the time, to everyone, about everything."

But then again, underneath the cynicism, he still believed that the truth was something to hope for, something to hold on to. Because in a world with no mercy and little justice, sometimes the truth was all you got.

***

Going south across the border a couple of hours later, it was about ten minutes before LaFleur realized he'd driven past the duty free shop without stopping. No peach schnapps for Arlene's Zombie this time. He'd been distracted, going over what he'd learned—and not learned—that morning.

His interview with Dufresne, Armand Broussard's regular gold buyer, had—as expected—led to nothing. Dufresne's jewelry shop was on the good side of the bad side of Kingston, classy enough to attract legitimate customers with disposable income, but seedy enough to attract a lot of gold sellers as well. He and Broussard had had a good business relationship, and while not exactly close friends, had known one another for several years. Dufresne had also assured LaFleur that the sensationalistic stories he'd heard about the craziness in the gold buying business were vastly overblown. There had only been that one bizarre case in Toronto, that business about the hit man, and that had turned out to be more media hysteria than anything else. No one was ever convicted. And no one in Kingston dressed in strange costumes and jumped around on street corners. Not in Kingston.

LaFleur became convinced that there wasn't enough money in the scrap gold business to motivate serious theft, much less a murder. A few thousand dollars, at most, in a month, even at current inflated prices. Just not enough money in it.

Karin had told him about the shipment Jimmy was taking to Kingston. And about Val Bondurenko's uncle, Lev? There was something here he was missing.

Time to talk to Karin again.

Skin in the Game

Lev was sitting across from Vasily in the library. Since Lev could not travel to Canada, for reasons he had never quite revealed, even to Vasily, it had been Vasily who had done all of the initial face-to-face negotiations with their buyer, Arkady Semilovich. Since the plutonium sample had been transported across the border separately, it had been no problem for Vasily to drive up to meet with Semilovich on several occasions. These meetings had all taken place in a small village on the outskirts of Kingston, which by a strange coincidence was called Odessa. Lev took this as a very good omen.

Lev picked up one of several disposable cell phones sitting on the desk and dialed Semilovich, using one of the several safe contact numbers he had been provided. "Arkady? It is Lev."

Semilovich did not often work with small-time operators like Lev Bondurenko, but if what Lev was promising was actually going to play out, Semilovich was glad to make an exception. He had some history with Lev, as well, back in Ukraine, which had been very profitable. And even though Lev had made some fairly serious misjudgments in the past—his dealings with Mendelokov, for example—Semilovich had learned that he could be trusted. He was even willing to allow Lev the privilege of North American-style first name only informality.

"Hello, Lev. Good to hear from you. I have been expecting your call."

"Yes. So, today you will get the sample we talked

about. You have your chemist there to confirm, yes?"

"Yes, Lev. We are ready and waiting."

"Good. My son Valentyn will be there soon." He really did think of Valentyn as a son, he thought; Arkady will trust him more, too.

"As I said, we are waiting. And if it proves genuine, then we will expect full delivery as soon as possible. You have complete confidence that the product can be delivered safely and in good time?"

"Absolutely, Arkady."

"Excellent. Then we are agreed, we go ahead."

"Good, good. Now, Arkady, there is another thing I would like to discuss with you."

"Yes, Lev, what is it?"

"It is a simple thing, really," Lev explained carefully, "something advantageous to us both." He paused, weighing his words. Arkady remained silent, waiting for Lev to continue.

Lev had given this a lot of thought. The money from the stock manipulation—about five hundred thousand invested, for an expected profit of anywhere from three to five million—compared to what this deal could bring, well, it had started to seem rather insignificant. Aside from the fact that he would be repaying Mendelokov for his and Petro's ruination, the stock deal had become secondary, in purely monetary terms, that is. Nothing could ever truly settle the debt owed him by Mendelokov; the money he would take from him was just a token. Mendelokov would be hurt, yes, but only marginally. Nothing this small could take down someone like Mendelokov. So the plutonium deal had slowly become, in Lev's mind, even more important than what Val and Fedir would engineer in Toronto.

"Yes, well, Arkady," Lev continued, "rather than being just a courier, for a fee—a very generous fee, I admit,"— *not really, Lev thought*—"I have been thinking that it would be better for both of us if I was more…invested in the operation. Better if I had 'skin in the game,' to use the American expression."

"Well, Lev, that is not so simple, actually. Are you sure you are willing—and able—to take that kind of risk? And in what amount are we talking, Lev?"

"I propose to provide one tenth of the required investment. That is two million of the twenty million needed to make the purchase. All I ask in return is a share in the return that is proportional to my contribution. And I pay for the two gram sample, the sample you will see soon. I buy this small piece, and the rest, you take."

"You have the money to do what you are proposing, Lev?" Arkady asked.

"I will have the money in my hands very shortly."

"But it is not 'in your hands' now? This does not sound good to me, Lev."

"There is nothing to worry about, Arkady. I promise you, I will have the money."

There was a pause while Arkady considered Lev's offer. It was not like two million dollars was a lot of money; but in principle, spreading the risk was good practice. And for a return of two hundred million, he would be giving up a relatively small percentage of the profit, only ten percent, but cut his exposure in equal measure. And it would create an obligation on Lev's part that could be very useful in the future. If Lev didn't produce? Well, that could be dealt with any number of ways.

"Let me think about it a moment, Lev."

"Certainly. But you would not be sorry, Arkady."

"You are right about that, Lev. If everything did not go exactly right, I would certainly *not* be the one to be sorry." He paused to let Lev consider the implications.

"There is no need to worry, "Lev said. "As we have discussed previously, the rest of the material is ready. I am prepared to deliver it."

"Very good. Now, as to your proposal: as soon as you

can verify for me that you have the money 'in hand,' as you say, we can finalize arrangements. To be clear: you are putting up two million dollars, one tenth of the purchase price of twenty million. Your share of the profit, after the final sale, is twenty million. This is correct?"

"Yes, Arkady."

"You will soon receive detailed instructions regarding how to transfer your portion of the funds. Then we will discuss the final delivery and payment details."

"Certainly, Arkady."

"Goodbye for now, Lev."

"Goodbye, Arkady. And thank you." If Lev's hand was shaking as he set down the phone, he was able to conceal it from Vasily.

"Vasily!" he called. "Champagne."

RAD MEDS

As soon as he got home, Jimmy tried to call Val again. No answer. He left two messages, both the same; *I have to talk to you, now*.

As he waited for Val to call him back, he became increasingly agitated over the scene he'd seen play out at the Ukrainian's apartment. And three beers after he'd gotten home hadn't stopped him from imagining that his hand was still burning. At one point he'd panicked a little and ran cold water on it. Even looked at it closely; *was that a red spot*?

Sonofabitch.

He tried to call Val for the third time. Again no answer. Left another message. *Call me.*

He looked at the spot on his hand again. Well, okay, maybe there was nothing there. But still.

As he'd been driving back down from Canada, he'd started putting things together, or at least thought he was.

First, there was the radioactive material in the bag, the one he'd first delivered to Lev, then had taken to Canada; the guy in Kingston hadn't paid much attention to it, but had still checked it. They must have some reason for sending it up there. And it was radioactive, for Chrissake. And not going to any goddam hospital in Kiev.

Second, he'd had all afternoon to Google various aspects of radioactive materials. After spending a considerable amount of time with Wikipedia, he thought he knew what was in that locket.

And it scared him.

***

"About time you called," was how he answered his phone when Val finally called late that afternoon.

Val hadn't tried to explain anything in detail over the phone, but assured Jimmy—had tried to assure Jimmy—that everything was okay. He'd explain everything when they met. He'd call back soon.

A couple of hours and several beers later, and no Val, Jimmy had had even more time to contemplate his situation.

Val had lied.

Lev had lied.

They had duped him into smuggling something really dangerous into Canada.

He was a fool.

What the hell am I doing with my life?

He hadn't realized how badly he'd screwed everything up until today. He wondered if there was some way he could make it up to Karin. It was too late to make it up to his father, of course.

He wasn't stupid. He'd always done well in school. Even thought about going to the technical institute in Rochester; his high school counselors had said he had an aptitude for engineering, and his grades were pretty good.

Where the hell was Val?

He'd tried to call Karin as soon as he got home, but she never answered her phone when she was on duty, and he didn't have a message ready when the voice mail had kicked in; voice mail always left him feeling like he was being tested—quick, tell me what you want, what you know, what I need to know, *now*. Like an oral pop quiz. He decided he'd better text her. He didn't know yet exactly what was wrong but he knew it was bad. He got out his iPhone and brought up iMessage.

KARIN. V & F BAD STUFF GOING DOWN. HOT GOLD. DBL CROSS. RAD MEDS. NOT SURE WHT IT ALL MEANS. TALK LATR.

He looked at the palm of his hand, then got up and got another beer.

Not Exactly

Karin came in and sat down at a table in the front corner of the restaurant, Doctor's Corner—the same table where she'd met LaFleur a few days earlier. It seemed like weeks.

LaFleur came out from the back; he'd seen her at the front door. "Thanks for coming over," he said, setting down a cup of coffee for her, and one for him, then pulling out a chair and sitting down across from her.

"Not at all," said Karin. "I was going to call you anyway."

"Oh?"

"Well, yes. It's about Jimmy, and Val, and—" She closed her eyes. "Mr. LaFleur, I think Val, I mean, Jimmy, well, Jimmy and Val—" She trailed off, tearing open a packet of sugar and dumping it in to her coffee.

LaFleur had long ago learned to not to hurry these things. He waited a few moments, and then gently prompted: "And?"

Karin stirred her coffee, obviously trying to compose herself. She reached over and picked up the pitcher of cream, then set it back down. "I don't use cream," she said, as if apologizing.

"I do," he said, and poured some into his coffee. He watched the cream swirl in fantastic patterns as he waited for Karin to continue.

"I'm worried about Jimmy, Mr. LaFleur. He sent me a text last night, and before that, there were the thefts at the hospital, and then I—"

"Slow down," LaFleur interrupted. "One thing at a time." Karin nodded. "Let's start with the hospital. Thefts?"

"Yes. From the radiological storeroom. Where radioactive isotopes are kept. Someone broke in—well, someone got into the storeroom—and stole several items. Radioactive materials used for tests, mainly. But it wasn't a break-in; someone used my key card for access."

"Your key card?"

"Yes. I'm pretty sure it must have been Val."

"Valentyn Bondurenko?"

"Yes."

"Your...boyfriend?" LaFleur hated the term "significant other," and took a chance that "boyfriend" wouldn't insult her.

"Well, yeah. At least I thought he was, well, serious. About us. But I haven't known him very long, I guess, and the thought that he could do something like this, well, I guess I didn't expect it. But now I think there is something even worse going on."

"Which is?"

"I got a text from Jimmy. I was on duty. I usually keep my phone turned off at the hospital, but when I got home and checked, there was this text. Something about Val and Fedir."

"Related to the thefts at the hospital?" LaFleur asked, trying to connect the dots.

"No, not exactly," Karin said. LaFleur repressed a reaction—he'd come to hate the phrase "not exactly." It seemed that everyone used it as a hedge against facing the truth. "At least, I didn't think so at first," she went on, hesitantly. "But I overheard some conversations between Val and Fedir at Val's apartment—they didn't know I'd come in—and I heard them talking, mostly in Ukrainian, but some English, and I could make out some of what they were talking about. They were using the Russian terms for radioactive isotopes, I'm sure—they aren't that much different than the English. And then I got that text from Jimmy, and I really started worrying. And I haven't been able get in touch with him since."

"What did he text?"

"Here," Karin said, reaching into her purse and pulling out a piece of notepaper. "I wrote it down. It doesn't make much sense."

LaFleur took the slip of paper, squinted at it, then pulled a pair of reading glasses out of his shirt pocket and tried again. "V & F. Val and, his brother, what is his name again?"

"Fedir."

"Yeah, Fedir, you just said that, sorry. Jimmy was in with them, right? Working with them on something? And now, he says it's gone bad?"

"Yes, I think so." She sipped at her coffee, looking at him over the rim of the cup.

There's more to this, he thought. He held up the note. "It goes on, 'hot gold;' what does that mean?" he asked. "The scrap gold? That was all legitimate, I thought. Nothing stolen."

"Yes, of course it was legitimate. That's what doesn't make sense, at least that part of it."

"But something here *does* make sense to you?" LaFleur asked.

"Now it does. After thinking about the way Val acted after I lost my key card."

"That key card that opens the door to the radiological supply room?"

"Yes, among other things. A few of us have access. My card was used while I wasn't on duty. I'm still trying to explain it to the hospital administrator. Unsuccessfully, so far. Since I don't really have a good answer."

"What was stolen?"

"Just some radiological tracers, materials used in

testing, mainly, isotopes used in cancer treatments. Nothing too dangerous. It breaks down quickly, that's why it's used in medical tests. I can't imagine what anyone would want it for."

LaFleur raised his eyebrows in sudden comprehension. "I get it; 'RAD MEDS' are radiation meds. That's what was stolen from the hospital. Radioactive isotopes."

"Right."

"And Jimmy was involved in this?"

"I guess so. And another thing: I think I told you he wanted to make the delivery to Canada, the regular gold trade Dad did every month. For some reason he wanted to do that right away. He wouldn't really tell me why. It was just the regular deal, taking the stuff up to Dufresne in Kingston. I'm sure he would have understood that we couldn't do it now, not under the, the circumstances."

"But that doesn't explain 'hot gold,' does it," LaFleur said.

"I know," said Karin. "I was hoping you'd be able to figure that out."

"Tell me more about what you heard at Val's apartment," LaFleur said. "The radioisotopes. What do you think is going on?"

She squeezed her eyes closed. "I don't know," she said. "I don't know."

"Karin, there's something funny going on here. You've got to help me figure out what that is. And—and this is something I think is a stretch at this point—if whatever is going on has anything to do with the murder of your father."

"I know. Things have gotten very strange in the past few days. I don't know what to think about Val anymore."

LaFleur sat back and rubbed at the two-day stubble on his jaw. There had to be something here, something key that Karin knew, or could lead him to. "Just think back over the past few days. Have you noticed anything else out of the ordinary? Anything unusual? Any changes, any variations in schedule, behavior? Anything other than the conversation you overheard."

"Val has definitely been more distant. Very cold. I've never been close to Fedir. He's always that way."

"Nothing you can think of that could explain their interest in the radioactive material?"

"No. What could they want with that stuff?"

"That's the question. Assuming it was them." He paused. "What about their recent activities? Anything new?"

"They spend a lot more time at Lev's. I think Jimmy has been going up there, too. This thing about the gold delivery, that has me really confused."

"You said Jimmy mentioned something about doing it for Lev, that Lev had some interest in the gold business?"

"Yes, but I don't understand why it has to be done now. Can't it at least wait until—?"

She broke off, fluttering her hands in front of her.

"I understand," LaFleur said. "You're distressed. For good reason. Take a few minutes to calm down, then we can start again. Want another cup of coffee? Maybe an Irish coffee, how does that sound? I have a special technique; learned it from a bartender in Dublin."

Karin smiled at LaFleur's earnestness, which was irresistible. "Yes, thanks, that would be wonderful."

He returned a few minutes later with two foaming cups. He waited until she'd taken a sip, then pressed on as he saw her relax a bit. "What about anything at Val's apartment? Have you seen anything else there that looked suspicious? Any reason to think he's hiding something there?"

She took another sip of Irish coffee, slurping up a bit of the whipped cream. "This is really good," she said. "Just what I needed." LaFleur nodded thanks. "Anything he's hiding...?" she repeated slowly.

"Or any reason to think there's something there that

could help explain what's going on?"

"I don't know. Well, maybe. He keeps a laptop, but not the one he normally uses, back in a bedroom closet. I've seen him stash it away in there when I've come in sometimes. Like I said, it's not his regular computer. But I've wondered about that before. Why he keeps it hidden in that closet."

"Do you think we could get a look at it?" LaFleur asked. "Not something I would normally ask, but, well, this 'hot gold' text has me worried. And as for your suspicions—I think a bit of unorthodox investigation may be in order here." He hoped he wasn't getting in too deep. As usual.

Karin hesitated before answering, "I suppose I could try to sneak it out of the apartment for a short time."

Peering over his Irish coffee, LaFleur said, "I think I need to talk to my friend Blueray."

Special Delivery

There had been no further word from Val. Jimmy was getting a little frantic. He was almost done texting another message to Karin—more carefully and more detailed this time—telling her everything he suspected, when he heard a knock at the door. He slipped the iPhone into his pocket; it must be Val, finally. He'd send Karin the message later, or call her if he found out more.

"God damn it, Val, where the hell have you been?" he said, jerking the door open.

"Calm, Jimmy, we need calm," Val said quietly as he came in. Fedir followed a few seconds later.

"Calm. Yeah, right." Jimmy had rehearsed two or three variations of his confrontation with Val, but now it was reduced to simple sarcasm. "Right."

"What is the problem, Jimmy? Everything went well, yes? You had no problems at the border. You called and said all was okay. So what is the problem?"

"You tell me, Val. You tell me what the goddam problem is. I don't know. I just know you've been lying to me. And Lev has been lying to me. What did you have me take into Canada, Val?"

"Jimmy, I told you. Medical test material, radiation treatments, for Kiev hospital."

"Bullshit. Guy in Kingston said there wasn't any hospital. Laughed. So, no hospital."

"Jimmy, you think we tell him everything? He's just a guy we use. My dumb cousin, Pavlo. A second cousin. He gets paid a little bit to do little things for us. Maybe he thinks he is more important than he really is."

"He seemed to know quite a bit. Said there would be a lot of money. Said there was a big deal going down. What deal, Val?"

Val looked down at the floor at this, obviously not happy to hear that the Kingston connection had been talking too freely.

"He is an idiot. I tried to tell Lev—well, never mind, that is not important. He does not know what he is saying. There is no 'big money,' only what we need to cover costs, and to deliver these medical supplies to Kiev. Only that."

Jimmy rubbed his eyes in bleary frustration. "I don't buy it, Val. Don't buy it," he said. "I overheard some things. Lev was making some kind of deal, and it wasn't about any medical supplies. And that scrap gold, the stuff I had to show that guy. What is the deal with that? I saw him take a big golden cross out of the box before he gave it back to me."

He noticed a shadow on the floor, appearing from behind him. He glanced back. It was just Fedir; he'd wandered into the kitchen and was just coming back out.

"What do you mean?" asked Val. "It was just a piece of jewelry—a family, um, treasure? A relative in Kiev, she asked for it. It has family connections. It used to belong to Shashen'ka. We send it with you so we don't have to pay tax, um, what is it, customs duty."

Jimmy scowled, confused, and distracted by Fedir moving up closer behind him. "But you'd pay duty in the Ukraine, not in Canada, right? Why would you—"

That reminded Jimmy of something else he'd thought about on the trip home. "Oh, yeah, about customs, the customs pass," he said. "How did you get that to work?" He was thinking back to the earlier meeting, when he'd asked Val this same question. He didn't get an answer then either. "Don't they have some sort of database or something? That they check against? They have barcodes on them, they scanned them." Jimmy had thought of this briefly at the border crossing; he'd been afraid the pass wasn't going to work, that there'd be questions. When everything went smoothly, he'd let out a huge sigh of relief as he'd driven away, and in his relief hadn't thought about it again, until now.

"You don't need to worry about that now, Jimmy," said Val. "It worked, right?"

"Yeah, but my pass, how was the barcode—" He stopped short of saying what had suddenly come to him. *Had the border officer used the name Armand?* He felt a cold pit form in the center of his stomach.

"We know how to fix these things, Jimmy," said Val. "You should not worry so much. You did a good job for us, now that is done; and you delivered the cross for us, an extra job we asked you to do, and we will show our appreciation."

The mention of the cross caused Jimmy to momentarily forget the customs pass, and he again imagined the palm of his hand burning. "You still haven't told me what it *really* was, Val," said Jimmy, beginning to panic. "It was not just a cross. I looked at it before I got there. I picked the goddam thing *up*."

"You picked it up," Val said, flatly.

"Yeah. And you know what, Val? *It burned my fucking hand.*"

Val saw Fedir's big black eyebrows shoot up like two caterpillars being launched into space. He held out his hands, trying to calm Jimmy down. "Now, Jimmy, I think you are dreaming things."

"I am not *dreaming* things. I don't know what the deal is with the medical crap; I know it's not going to Kiev, but the other thing, that cross. That thing is *dangerous*, man. I saw what the guy did with it, there was something hidden inside it; he was crapping his pants just getting it out of the box. And I've heard Lev talking to someone about this stuff. I checked some things out online. It wasn't that hard to figure out, Val. It's fucking *plutonium*. Bad ju-jus, man. And now it's all making sense, what I overheard, before. Not about the hospital meds, but about plutonium. I heard Lev talking about plutonium. Lev is selling it on the black market, isn't he?"

"You've told someone about this?" Val asked, calmly, ignoring Jimmy's questions.

Jimmy edged back a step, almost bumping into Fedir, who shifted back a step as well.

"No. No, Val, of course not." Jimmy held out his hand. "Val, it *burned* me."

"Jimmy, that's crazy. It was just a religious icon, nothing more."

"What are you doing, Val? Are you terrorists?" His eyes bulged in sudden fear as he said this.

The brass weight in Fedir's hand came down on the back of Jimmy's skull with a soft thud, like a brick dropped into wet concrete. Jimmy's eyes rolled back into his head and he fell in a heap at Val's feet.

As Jimmy hit the floor, the iPhone came out of his pocket and skittered across the floor.

"Pick up the phone, Fedir," Val commanded.

Fedir slipped the shiny brass weight back into his jacket pocket as he bent down to get Jimmy's phone. He held it up to show Val the screen.

"There's a text message on the screen," he said.

"Give it to me," Val said irritably. He looked down at Jimmy as Fedir handed him the phone. *Was he dead? Goddam Fedir. How were they going to explain this to Lev? He was already angry enough.*

As Val raised the phone up to look at the message, he heard a small *beep*.

"God damn it, what was that?"

Fedir leaned over to look. The message had disappeared. "Stupid."

"Shut up, Fedir."

Val quickly thumbed commands on the phone, trying to figure out what had just happened.

Suddenly he jerked his head up to look at Fedir.

"Great, Fedir. Just great. You just killed Jimmy, probably," Val said, tapping Jimmy's body with his foot, "and we just sent a text message to Karin telling her about the plutonium."

Fedir frowned.

"That's not good, Val," he said.

"No, Fedir. Not good."

"What are we going to do?" Fedir asked, looking around the room, as if he expected to see an answer written on the walls.

"Just bring the van around to the back of the house, Fedir" he said, kneeling down to look closely at Jimmy's face. Jimmy was not breathing.

"Shit, Jimmy," he said softly. "Why did you suddenly have to get so smart?"

I Was Never Here

Raymond "Blueray" Levin was one of those whiz kids you hear about, never more than two seconds away from a computer, tablet, or iPhone, and able to fix anything from a laptop to a DVR to a dedicated server. He was in constant demand as a technical support geek by his mother's friends, who all thought themselves to be computer-literate but in reality didn't even know how email worked—they thought it was like turning on the water in the kitchen sink, it was just there. And they all thought Blueray was a "dream"—smart, young, good-looking, with a Josh Groban haircut and Elvis eyelashes—and were constantly trying to get him to date their daughters, or granddaughters.

But Blueray had other things to do. He could do about anything computer or web related; he was a real natural. He'd had some exposure to computer science and IT courses, but only informally, and as a maverick—while auditing some courses at SUNY, he'd driven the professors crazy, wondering where this kid had learned so much before he'd shown up, often unannounced, in their classes.

LaFleur had sort of adopted Blueray after their previous experience together in tracking down the arsonist. Blueray's parents had split soon after LaFleur met him, practically abandoning him, and they had done not much for him before that point, either, as far as LaFleur could tell—so LaFleur had been helping him with expenses. Least he could do; he figured some of what Blueray had done for him on the arson case had probably saved his life. Well, maybe that was stretching it, but still. He owed the kid.

Since Blueray had worked for LaFleur before, he was not too surprised when he got the call, even if it was practically the middle of the night. What did surprise him was the nature of the request.

"Whose laptop? And why?" Blueray asked.

"Listen, just don't ask, okay?" said LaFleur. "Plausible deniability, right?"

Blueray held the phone away from his ear, frowning, trying to figure out what LaFleur was up to. "Blueray?" he heard, faintly.

He put the phone back to his ear, still a bit bemused, but intrigued. "Ummm. 'Plausible deniability,' huh? Okay, that sounds almost irresistibly interesting."

"How soon can you be here?"

***

They wouldn't have much time, Karin warned. She could predict Val's schedule—that was no problem, he wouldn't be home for at least an hour—but she wasn't as sure about Fedir; he seemed to come and go at odd hours. Blueray assured her he wouldn't need more than about fifteen minutes. "I've seen the kid work," LaFleur assured her. "He's a wizard."

It took Karin only a few minutes to get from LaFleur's car, where they'd been sitting—she had followed them over in her car, and they'd parked a block away—into the apartment and back with the laptop.

Blueray flipped open the top and groaned. LaFleur looked over with an alarmed look on his face. "What?"

"You didn't tell me it was a *Russian* laptop," said Blueray. "The keyboard—it's in the Cyrillic alphabet. Very uncommon."

"I didn't know. Is that a problem?"

"Wouldn't be, if I knew more Russian. But I think I can

recognize some of the characters, the ones that are not already Roman analogues, that is. But, hey, I love a challenge."

As soon as the computer powered up, Blueray turned to Karin. "Okay. Password. What's his birthday?"

"Um, July, uh, fifteenth."

"Year?"

"Oh, well. Let's see, he said he was twenty-eight, so, that's what—"

"Nineteen eighty-five," said Blueray, instantly. He tapped on the keyboard. Keyboard numbers were easy. He tried several permutations.

"Nope," he said after a minute. "Any important names in his life? Mother, father…?"

"No, he never mentions them; I think he was raised by his uncle. Lev," she said, turning to LaFleur.

"No chance you'd know his birthday?" said Blueray.

"No."

"Is 'Lev' short for anything?"

"I don't think so."

"Well, I don't know what those characters would be, nothing looks obvious. Anyway, that's too short. Anything else you can think of?"

Karin looked back over at Blueray. "He talks about his aunt a lot—Lev's wife—well, she died—but I think they were very close. Her name was Shashen'ka."

Blueray bent low over the laptop. "Which one of these 'S' looking things do you suppose is 'S?'" he asked, talking to himself. He tapped keys steadily for three or four minutes. "Bingo," he said, popping his head up and grinning. "Not what I thought at first. 'S' looks like a 'C.' Must be something I saw once and stored it away subconsciously. Also had some upper/lower case thing going, but not too sophisticated. Pretty weak password."

"Told you," LaFleur said to Karin.

Blueray poked around the file system for a couple of

minutes, getting a feel for what was there. Then he turned to LaFleur, smiling. "Now, to work," he said, pulling a USB flash drive out of his pocket and slipping it into the port on the side of the computer.

A few seconds later, LaFleur had to look over in alarm again, as Blueray gave out with a long, drawn out, "Whaaaat?" He flicked his eyes up at LaFleur. "No worries, just a small glitch." He bent back over the keyboard. "Need to muck with the default page encoding before my program runs on the machine, to deal with these fonts correctly. I can't pull anything off of the drive otherwise."

"I was going to suggest that," said LaFleur, drily.

"You could have said something sooner," Blueray said, laughing. A few seconds later, he pulled the thumb drive from the USB slot. "Okay, just let me clean up my tracks, then we're done." He tapped at the keyboard for another few minutes, then powered off the machine.

"All set," he said, turning to Karin. "Get this thing back where it belongs." He turned to LaFleur, handing him the drive. "I don't think we'll have any problems reading the files. From what I saw before I did the scrape of the disk, I don't think there was any serious encryption, and everything appears to be readable. We should look in particular at emails, spread sheets. Other documents—if there is too much in Russian, or Ukrainian, whatever, we might have a problem. We can also look for browser history and temporary internet files; that won't be hard at all, and can tell you a lot about what they have been doing. People are usually very sloppy about cleaning up after themselves."

"Great, thanks. Can you come over first thing tomorrow morning? I want to get cracking on this."

"Sure," said Blueray. "And A.C.?"

"Yeah?" LaFleur answered.

"I was never here."

***

Karin left LaFleur and Blueray in their car and hurriedly replaced the laptop on the shelf in Val's closet. She'd told LaFleur she'd stay and wait for Val to come home; maybe she could learn something more. LaFleur had argued against it—too dangerous, he said, and besides, they all needed some sleep—and she finally relented. She waved to him as she walked back to her car, and he and Blueray drove off.

On the way back to her apartment, she went over and over what was happening, trying to make sense out of even the smallest part of it. She knew Val had no reason to suspect she had overheard anything, or that she suspected something was going on, no matter that she had only a vague idea of what it could be. She tried to think back on what she'd heard. She also went back to the last time she'd seen Jimmy, and tried to remember if he'd said anything that could be related to the radioisotope thefts.

No, that was crazy. Jimmy might be doing something for Lev, but he'd said it was only about scrap gold.

But his text had mentioned 'rad meds'—that could only mean radioactive medical substances. Could Jimmy really be involved?

She had to find Jimmy.

Bar Hopping

Just as Karin walked into her apartment, her phone buzzed; a text had come through. By the time she had finished reading it, her hands were shaking. She could barely dial LaFleur's cell number.

There was no answer. He wasn't expecting a call, she realized, especially since she'd agreed to go straight back to her apartment, not stay at Val's. When his voice mail picked up, she left a message for him to call her right away; that she'd had another text from Jimmy, and it was worse than they'd thought. She was so flustered that she did not give him any details about the text, just said again that it was urgent.

She turned and almost ran back out of the apartment.
Oh, my God. Plutonium. Dirty bomb. Oh, my God.
She almost screamed.
Where's Jimmy?

***

First she tried the Port Tavern over on Lake, up by SUNY. For some reason she knew "the Port" was where Jimmy did most of his hanging out, but couldn't remember where she'd heard that; maybe he'd mentioned it at some point. It was as dismal inside as she'd expected it to be: dark and damp, with a dissolute looking couple in a seedy booth, three customers at the bar, one with his head face down, a half glass of beer in front of him. She tried not to picture Jimmy in that state. She still had more faith in him than that. In spite of—well, she just had to find him; there must be some explanation.

She decided to start over again on the East side; there were two places to check out over there, and a place to park. After leaving her car in the lot at East First Street, she went across the street into G.S. Steamers in the Quality Inn. It was much more upscale than the Port Tavern, with a large central bar and a great terrace along the waterfront. She went all the way around the bar, then out to the terrace. Not surprisingly, no Jimmy. She went back outside and started down the street towards the Captain's Quarters, and was almost there before she remembered they didn't have a bar. She turned around and trudged back up to Bridge.

Crossing over the bridge to the west side, she pulled her coat closely around her, crossing her arms in front of her and bending away from the wind coming up the river. There were several bars over there, she knew, on West Bridge, and more on Water.

Across the bridge, just past W. First Street, she came to The Alley Cat. *Sounds like Jimmy's kind of place*, she thought. She ducked in and looked around, ignoring the stares of the barflies and the puzzled looks from the few regular-looking patrons at the tables. It was not a bad looking place, considering, with a huge aquarium behind the bar that lit the whole room in shimmering, aquamarine light. But no Jimmy.

This was getting tedious.

Going back out onto Bridge Street, she tried to remember how far up the street the next bar was, but this was not a part of town she spent a lot of time in. She decided she'd try down on Water, instead, and then double back up farther west on Bridge if she had to. She also started to regret walking over to this side of the river, dreading the walk back to her car. *God damn him, anyway.*

She went back down Bridge and turned right on Water, heading towards Cayuga. On the river side was a bar and restaurant called The Old City Hall. She crossed over and went in. She'd been there before and remembered it as a nice place: great food, good people. It was crowded, just as she remembered it; it took her a few minutes to work her way through the crowd, but it soon became obvious that Jimmy wasn't here either.

She went back out onto Water and looked around. There was another place across the street that she wasn't familiar with, Club Crystal. It looked dark and foreboding. *Oh, well.* Club Crystal turned out to be as dark and foreboding inside as out, and had very few customers. Maybe things didn't pick up here until much later, she decided. Anyway, still nothing. Maybe she should just go home and try to call Mr. LaFleur again, she thought.

Back out on the street, she was uncertain about which way to go—back out to Bridge or over to Cayuga—and thought she'd have to go all the way around the block, but then noticed the small alley next to Club Crystal, heading west; she could cut through to First that way.

Still silently cursing Jimmy for a fool, not paying much attention to where she was going, and not being able to see much in the dark, she almost ran into someone standing in the alley in front of her. She gasped involuntarily, and stumbled back a foot or two, trying to make out the figure in front of her.

She could see that it was a man, but he seemed to be wearing something over his head, a hood, or a mask? He stepped forward, closing in on her.

She couldn't think. Her heart was pounding. She knew she had to do something but felt frozen in place. The man moved another step closer, and she could now see that he was wearing a black balaclava that completely covered his face. His hand came out of his pocket, and she caught a glint of something metallic, she couldn't tell what.

Suddenly a door in the back wall of Club Crystal opened; it was almost hidden by two fire escape stairways, but still flooded the alley with yellow light. A skinny young kid stood in the doorway holding a bucket of trash. The man in the balaclava thrust his hand back into his pocket, then turned and ran the other direction, up the alley, up the steps at the end, and out onto First Street..

But not before Karin saw the man's eyes, lit up by the light from the doorway like a cat's.

Fedir.

***

She ran all the way to her car. Out of breath, she sat at the wheel for a minute or two, trying to calm down.

There was a winter survival kit in the trunk—some clothes, power bars, water, flashlight, a blanket. She could run. Hide.

Hands trembling, she started the car and pulled out onto Second, then turned left onto Bridge and drove east out of town, as fast as she dared.

Her hands didn't stop shaking until she'd gotten onto I-81 at Pulaski, heading north half an hour later. At Watertown, she turned east again, onto state highway 126.

It was almost dawn when she pulled into the parking lot of the Olympic Dream Lodge and Cottages, just a few blocks from the center of Lake Placid. There were no lights showing in any of the cabins, or in the main office. Which cabin had it been? She couldn't remember.

She'd never quite known what it was that had happened between her and Michael. They had been seeing one another regularly, and had had a wonderful time up here, a couple of years ago. Then he'd suddenly gotten cold feet. He'd tried to explain, had started to tell her about something that had happened to him that made it difficult for him to get close, to commit, but he could never get past that point. She'd been disappointed, but eventually understood that Michael was struggling with something she couldn't help with. Then she'd met Val. *Dear God, what is happening?*

She got out of the car and took the blanket out of the trunk. Back in the car, she spread the blanket over her, then leaned back and closed her eyes.

***

"Ma'am? Can I help you?"

Karin jerked awake at the tap on the window, squinting in the early morning light. She heard the muffled voice of a stranger peering in at her, a kindly looking older gentleman in a plaid shirt and a baseball cap with a large fish embroidered in bright yellow on the front.

She looked out at the man and burst into tears.

Wake Up Call

It was early morning, just before dawn. Lev liked to have coffee out on the back deck when the sun came up. It reminded him of the Black Sea. Every time Lev looked at the lake, he thought of the Black Sea.

Val and Fedir followed Vasily out on to the deck, interrupting Lev's reveries. He hated to have his morning routine broken. But he sat impassively while they related what had just happened, and what they'd done with Jimmy. What had happened with the phone.

Lev passed his coffee cup to Vasily for a refill. As he waited, he looked intently at Val and Fedir, now seated across from him. He did not know whether to be relieved or furious; he decided a bit of both. Relieved that he no longer had to rely on Jimmy, as Valentyn had never quite convinced him that Jimmy was reliable; but after what had happened to Armand Broussard, he had been forced to try. And furious that they had allowed Jimmy to not only learn so much about what they were doing, but had also allowed him to tell Karin. That was nearly inexcusable.

Lev looked out at the lake for a moment to calm himself, then turned back to them. "So, your friend Jimmy did not work out so good for us. This all could have worked very well. But no matter. Now we have to do what we need to do.

"You will go to Toronto, as we have planned. Everything is in place. But first, Valentyn, you will go to Kingston to get the materials you need, everything for Toronto, and the sample for Arkady Semilovich. You have nothing in the car, so no problem at the border, yes? Very important, Valentyn, I know I can trust you to do this." He turned to Fedir. "And, you, while Val takes care of things in Kingston, you take care of Karin. You must do this quickly, Fedir. Then you meet Val."

"But how can I find her?" Fedir asked. He held out his hands beseechingly. "We checked her apartment already; and her car is gone, she is not there."

"You still have Jimmy's phone, yes?" Lev asked sweetly.

"Yes, it is right here," Fedir said, pulling it out of his pocket.

"Well, then, ask her where she is."

"Oh," said Fedir. He held the phone up and started selecting icons on the screen, looking for Karin's number. He was about to press "dial" when Lev craned his neck over to see what he was doing.

"Text, Fedir! Not voice."

Fedir looked up guiltily.

"*Pah*," said Lev.

***

The phone's rude buzz startled Karin awake. She'd been asleep not even an hour, against her will, sitting in an Adirondack deck chair on the back porch of the cabin she'd rented. She had been so physically and emotionally exhausted that she hadn't been able to stay awake.

She hoped and prayed—and she never prayed—that this was LaFleur calling back, even as she dimly realized that the buzz had not been her normal ring tone, but the tone for a text message.

She suppressed a gasp as she saw the screen. A text from Jimmy: Whre are u?

She quickly typed back: Call me.

There was a long delay. She stared at the screen, willing characters to appear, for the phone to ring. Finally, another text appeared: Can not talk now. With Val.

There was another short delay, then a repeat of the first question: Karin Where are you?

She quickly typed her reply: Lake Placid. Olympic Dream Cottages. What is going on? Fedir followed me in Oswego last night. Scared. What is going on?

There was another slight delay, then another message: Can not talk now, I will come there wait for me.

She texted back, frantically now: Jimmy what is happening???

There was no answer.

***

After Fedir had texted Karin and they knew where she was, Lev repeated his instructions to them both and sent them away. He sat looking out at the lake.

This made things much more difficult.

The money from the stock market ploy was important for two reasons; he got back from Mendelokov what had been stolen from him, and it funded the plutonium deal. This he had confidence in; the plan had been set up very carefully; the stocks chosen would both be very sensitive to a quick market down turn, and losses would deeply hurt Mendelokov.

But the other matter was now severely compromised. He had been depending on Jimmy to get the remaining plutonium to his contact in Canada. The FAST track through Canadian customs would have been perfect. Now he would have to figure out all over again how to safely transport it across the border. Maybe that other jeweler, that Dufresne—maybe they would have to use him somehow after all. He could come here, pick up the stuff—he would not know what was hidden in it—and then Valentyn could deal with it on the Canadian side. Yes, maybe that would work. Or maybe a boat.

He was running out of time.

Plato's Beard

LaFleur woke up at about three A.M., wondering what was on the flash drive. He was also kept awake by the thought of what they'd actually done earlier that night; even with Karin's implicit permission, he'd had a hard time getting past the fact that there'd been no legitimate excuse for it—no warrant, no conceivable way to get a warrant—but in the end, he felt he had no choice. Wished he hadn't had to have pulled Blueray into it, at least not in the way he did.

Maggie barely moved when he got out of bed; he pulled the light blanket up over her and went into his office down the hall.

The first thing LaFleur saw after he booted up the computer was an email from Blueray; apparently he'd done some internet sleuthing as soon as he'd gotten home. What he'd found was disturbing. Lev Bondurenko had ties to at least two known mob groups based in Eastern Europe. He'd also been involved in a stock fraud instigated by the Ukrainian mobster Sergei Mendelokov, the leader of the so-called "Red Mafia," apparently as a victim. What was clear was the extent of Mendelokov's influence. The fraud had involved a U.S. energy company traded on the Toronto Stock Exchange. After the fraud was exposed by the FBI, the shares in the company became worthless overnight, costing investors over a billion dollars. It looked like Lev had been hurt badly.

Obviously, they'd need to take a closer look at all this. But based on what he'd just read he was more than convinced they had plenty to worry about.

***

Two hours later, LaFleur sat back from the computer—he had a bad habit of leaning in towards the screen when something captured his attention—and contemplated what to do next. Blueray's advice to look at Val's browsing history had been smack on. There were links to several financial institutions, and even though he'd been unable to login in, they were obviously trading accounts, mostly for the Toronto exchange, as far as he could tell. (Blueray could make short work of these accounts, he was sure, although he was reluctant to encourage something quite so blatantly, well, probably illegal.) There were several links to various sites related to the Toronto PATH underground—maps, transportation timetables, street views—along with a map saved as a JPEG and marked at various points with red circles.

There were links to sites related to radioactive materials of various kinds—all innocuous in themselves, reputable sources like the NRC, AEC, other organizations both public and private, along with information from Wikipedia, which he didn't completely trust but had led him to other solid information—including a link to an EPA "Plutonium Radiation Protection" page.

LaFleur had been bothered by the lack of motive since first talking with Karin—and this dissatisfaction had only been enhanced by his visits with Chief Boyko and Earl Dufresne—and had not been able to come up with anything himself. There just wasn't enough money in scrap gold to "justify" murder, and in a case like this, where there was no passion, no pre-meditation, no obvious financial motive. The original assumption had been that it was a simple burglary interrupted, the murder the result of panicked intruders. Which was exactly what LaFleur had been thinking all along. But he'd never been particularly comfortable with that assumption. The links to plutonium fact sheets and other pages he'd come across started him down a different path.

If there was no money in gold—enough money to interest Lev, in any case—there was certainly money in illicit plutonium. Probably big money.

He went back to Google and began searching for recent news related to plutonium thefts, accidents, unexplained incidents involving anything highly radioactive. It didn't take long.

The first item related to the mysterious appearance of a highly radioactive source in a shipping container sitting on a dock in Genoa, Italy. A routine inspection had detected high levels of radiation coming from the container. After moving the container to an isolated area of the docks and sealing it off from close approach, it sat for months while authorities tried to determine what to do with it—and what it contained. A nuclear bomb, even just a dirty bomb?

Finally, six months after it had first been detected, a robotic probe found a small cylinder of cobalt stuck in amongst the tons of other harmless scrap metal. The container's last known port of entry was Jeddah, Saudi Arabia.

There were some other references to various other incidents. One he thought amusing—in a twisted way—the report of a lost device used for evaluating fracking sites. The company responsible had apparently mislaid a cylinder containing an americium-241/beryllium neutron source. Not immediately deadly if you just happened across it, the company said. But the radioactive material in the cylinder was potentially—"though very unlikely," they stressed—fatal under the right circumstances. *This stuff is everywhere*, he thought.

***

While skimming the plutonium page earlier, he'd come across—though there was no way he could know this—exactly the same thing Jimmy had found earlier that day. Plutonium—a lump of plutonium 238, just sitting by itself—was hot. Thermally hot, not "hot" as in "stolen," which was what they'd assumed Jimmy meant by "hot jewelry." Plutonium 239—the type used in nuclear weapons—did not generate heat in the same way. Maybe this was good news.

He realized he was sitting there just staring at the screen, still unable to fully process what he'd been reading. He closed out of the browser and navigated back to a folder full of documents he'd passed over earlier. Anything with a Cyrillic name—displayed like garbage text on his computer—he skipped. There were, however, a set of spreadsheets with English names, file names like energystocks.xls, trades.xls, orders.xls. He opened one after another and browsed through them. He was unfamiliar with the stock names; they all seemed to be foreign energy stocks, probably Eastern European or Russian, he thought. A few were obviously Russian oil and energy company stocks. Lists of prices, what looked like target buy/sell prices, but nothing jumped out at him.

But where did Armand Broussard fit in?

He sat back and rubbed his eyes. Newton, seeing an opportunity open up—cats never really sleep, LaFleur had decided, they just lurk, looking like they are asleep—roused himself from the cushion he was napping on and levitated himself up onto LaFleur's lap.

"So, Newton, what do you think?" he asked, absently scratching Newton behind the ears. Newton's instant purr was gratifying, but didn't answer the question.

Too many questions. None of it made any sense.

He switched from Newton's ears to his chin and was rewarded with an even louder hum of satisfied approval. If only everything were as easy.

"Well, what do we have so far, Newt, old bean? Burglary gone badly isn't a bad assumption on the face of it; but why wouldn't they have gone through with it? Nothing was really missing, as far as Karin could tell. And with no alarm going off, there would have been time to take whatever they wanted." Newton looked up in agreement. "And why no alarm? Karin didn't think he'd forget to set it, though that must be what happened."

LaFleur shifted a bit, and Newton resettled. "And now we have the thefts from the hospital radiological supply room and the bizarre text from Jimmy. And the warning about the Bondurenkos. Put that together with what we've seen so far from Val's computer—we were perfectly justified in that, by the way—and what do we have?" Newton twitched. "Yeah, you're right. We've still got nothing."

Nothing that made sense, LaFleur reminded himself, *yet*. He'd seen it go like this many times. A jumble of information, no apparent connections. Jigsaw puzzle pieces were sitting there all around him, ready to be picked up and put into place, but he had mittens on.

He had great faith in a logical technique known as Occam's Razor—that the simplest explanation that fit all of the facts was probably the correct one—which had served well in that past. But LaFleur also remembered reading a philosophical article that referred to Occam's Razor and the problem of "nonbeing;" though this had not been the full import of the argument, LaFleur took it to mean, at least in part, that even *nothing* was *something*. The author had called this dilemma Plato's Beard. LaFleur sighed. The razor was a bit dull this morning. But still. Nothing can't mean, well, nothing. There must be something else there, something he was missing. Just have to look harder. The clues he needed were there, he was sure, and by eliminating the unnecessary—reducing the problem to the simplest elements, using Occam's Razor—*nothing* would become the *something* they were looking for. He began to drift off. *Nothing from nothing leaves nothing*; the tune ran through his head, triggering a cascade of old songs, half-remembered. *Nothing is easy. Nothing compares to you. Something in the way she moves.*

He raised his head and tried to focus. *Got to be something here I'm missing*, he thought again. He stretched, sat up in his chair, and leaned forward.

Just as he was about to dive back into the net, the phone rang.

Things Have Changed

"Slow down," LaFleur was saying, as Maggie walked into the office, after being awakened by the phone. Now she stood silently in the doorway listening to LaFleur's side of the call.

Newton jumped down from LaFleur's lap and walked over to Maggie and starting rubbing himself against her legs. LaFleur mouthed "Michael" to her as he listened. "Okay, got it. Be there in ten." He put the phone down gently, turning to Maggie with a grim look. "Jimmy Broussard's body has just been found."

"Oh, my God. Where?"

"An old barn over on Black Creek Road. Whoever dumped him there apparently thought the barn was abandoned—you know how some of those old farms out there look—well, the farmer went out to the barn to do something or other, some farm thing, I don't remember what Michael said. Anyway, not important. The coroner called Michael; they'd talked about the Broussard case at the hospital. And another thing: both Jimmy and his father appear to have been killed in the same way. The coroner thought he should give Michael a heads up."

"I heard you say 'be there in ten.' Where?"

"The morgue. Michael is on his way there now."

Maggie had a sudden thought. "What about Karin? Has she been notified?"

"Michael asked the coroner to wait until we got there before the police tried to contact Karin. He thought it would be best if someone she knows breaks the news, and, besides, maybe we'll know something more about it before we talk to her." LaFleur stood up and moved to the doorway.

"Can I come with you?" Maggie asked.

"You're best out of this one," he said, shaking his head. "I don't know what we're dealing with, yet, but it looks like a bad bunch. I'm not going to put you at risk again."

He gave her a quick kiss on his way out.

"I'll try not to be too long."

***

Michael was in the lobby waiting for him.

"Anything?" LaFleur asked as he walked in.

"Too early to know for sure, but looks like cause of death was a blow to the head."

LaFleur grunted. "Hunh. Why am I not surprised?"

"Yeah, I know what you mean."

"I guess no point in waiting around here, at least for now?"

Michael nodded. "I thought we could go over to Karin's together. Better than a phone call. Coroner cleared it with a Detective DeSalvo; he's the one who's working the case, coincidentally enough—he is also working the father's murder. Anyway, he agreed there's no need to bother the chief at this hour. And they don't like doing this kind of thing either."

LaFleur nodded. "Yeah. Not the best gig on earth."

Out in the parking lot, Michael steered LaFleur over to his Mercedes SLK. "I'll drive," he said.

LaFleur hesitated. "Can I fit into that thing?"

"Bigger than it looks."

LaFleur glanced back at his '89 Grand Am, then back at the Mercedes.

"Let's go."

***

There was no response to knocking or ringing the bell at Karin's apartment. LaFleur checked the parking lot and determined that her car wasn't there.

Michael called the hospital and confirmed she wasn't there, either; he'd been pretty sure she wasn't scheduled. He did manage, with some difficulty—not wanting to give away any information unnecessarily—to get Karin's cell number from the duty nurse. They walked back to Michael's car.

"I'll put it on speaker," Michael said, as he dialed Karin's cell.

"Hello? Who is this?" Karin answered.

"Karin, this is Michael Fuentes. I have Detective LaFleur here in the car with me. You're on speaker."

"Michael! What is going on? I just got a message from—"

"Karin, please hold on a minute. I'm afraid we have some bad news. Where are you? Are you close to home?"

"Oh, God, Michael, no, no I'm not in Oswego. I was out late last night trying to find Jimmy and—I was going to call you, Mr. LaFleur. Didn't you get my message on your cell?"

LaFleur cursed himself for a Luddite as he realized he had not, in fact, checked his cell voice mail before going to bed. He just wasn't as connected as most people seemed to be these days. "Sorry, no," was all he could manage.

"There was another message from Jimmy. It sounded bad. But I just woke up. Woke up again, I mean—"

"Karin," interrupted LaFleur, "where are you? Can we meet you somewhere?"

"Fedir followed me, downtown. I think he was going to attack me. I was afraid to go home. I just got in the car and drove here."

Sonofabitch, whispered LaFleur.

"Karin, one thing at a time. Where are you right now?"

"I'm in Lake Placid, a tourist cabin. Michael, you know, it's where we—where, where we—" She broke down, gasping, unable to go on.

Michael turned to LaFleur, mouthing "later." LaFleur raised his eyebrows but didn't say anything.

"Karin," LaFleur went on. "It's very important that we speak to you." He waited a second, and then asked, "Are you okay? Can you talk now?"

They heard snuffling noises, then Karin answered, voice quavering but under control. "Yes, yes, I can talk. But Mr. LaFleur, I just got a message from Jimmy, and he says he's coming here, he—"

"Karin! What did you just say? You got a message from Jimmy? When, Karin, last night?"

"No, just now, just this morning."

"Karin, no, that's not possible."

"But it was him, just a few minutes ago. He texted me and asked where I was and said he's coming here."

"Karin. I'm sorry, Karin, that could not have been Jimmy." He paused.

"What?"

"Karin, Jimmy was found earlier this morning. He'd been hit on the head and left in a barn out in the country."

"So, is he, is he okay, is he—"

"Karin, I'm so sorry." He paused. No other way. "Jimmy is dead, Karin."

There was a gasp, then Karin came back, loudly protesting, "No, no, no, he sent me a text message, just a few minutes ago, he's on his way here."

"Please, Karin. Listen to me. That could not have come from Jimmy. We just left the morgue. Jimmy could not have sent that message." Karin did not answer. "Karin, are you there?"

They sat in the car, staring at the phone in silence for what seemed like minutes. When Karin finally spoke, her voice was faint and low. Michael and LaFleur could barely hear her.

"Oh, my God. I just told Fedir where I am."

LaFleur and Michael looked at one another, trying to think of what to say next. Karin spoke first this time.

"He's going to kill me, isn't he? He killed Jimmy, now he's going to kill me. Oh, God. I have to get out of here. I'm going to—"

"Karin, wait a minute. Why do you think Fedir followed you? Did something happen between you and Val, or Fedir?"

"All I know, Mr. LaFleur, is that after what happened last night, and after what Jimmy told me, I can't stay here."

"What Jimmy told you? You mean in the text message, the one about the 'hot jewelry?' Listen, I think he meant—"

"Yes, I know. He sent me a second text. Or at least he tried; it looked like it got cut off. Jimmy said Val and Fedir have plutonium, not just the stuff from the hospital. He thinks they are going to plant a dirty bomb somewhere. Then Fedir followed me, and…Oh, God, Val is a terrorist. Oh, no." She started sobbing again.

"Hang on, Karin, hang on. Let us think about this."

It took a few seconds, but Karin got control of herself enough to respond with an "okay."

This changed things. LaFleur had spent the early morning hours learning quite a bit about what Val and Fedir—and Lev, he reminded himself—were up to, but with what Karin had just told him, he realized he may have been just scraping the surface. He immediately understood that Karin was not safe as long as she was in the area. They had already killed twice, and although he still didn't understand the details, he knew that this involved much more than a handful of scrap jewelry. Lev was not interested in the gold business, never had been. LaFleur had come to that realization as soon as he understood what Jimmy's first text message said. He suspected that Lev had the resources and the desire to track her down if she ran off again. Most people didn't realize how easily they could be tracked. Credit card purchases, phone location, even border crossings—LaFleur knew enough about what Blueray was capable of to know that they had to be very careful about how to proceed.

"Michael, I can't explain in detail right now, but based on what I've learned in the past few hours, and what Karin just told us, I believe she is in—" he didn't like the melodramatic sound of this, but it was true—"mortal danger."

"From what she just said, I believe it. Listen, I can be there in, what about three hours? I'll go get her and—"

"No good," LaFleur said bluntly. "Fedir has, what, at least a half an hour head start. He'd beat you there even in your car. And we can't have her just running off somewhere else. These guys are serious. We've got to get her someplace safe, with no way for Lev & Co. to track her down, at least not easily." He leaned over toward the phone, lying on the seat between them. "Karin? Still there?"

"Yeah, still here. I heard what you said."

"Good. Okay, just stay put for a few minutes. We'll call you right back as soon as we work out what to do to keep you safe, okay?"

"Okay. Um, you'll call me back, soon, right?"

"Sure, Karin, don't worry. Call you right back. Just hang on a few more minutes."

"But Fedir. He's coming here! He's on his way here now. I can't—" She broke down again.

"Okay, Karin, you're right. We've got to get you away from there. But we need you to be ready to move quickly once we get ready to move you, okay?"

"Uh, yes, okay," Karin replied, weakly.

"First thing, we move you away from the cottages. Just move your car to someplace out of the way, a parking lot behind a business, or off the side of the road with some tree cover, something like that. Do you think there is something close by like that?"

"Yes. Yes, I understand. I'll move the car."

"Okay. Not too far, though, until we know what we're going to do. Just someplace out of sight where you can leave it indefinitely and it won't be easily spotted by someone"—*Fedir*—"just driving by. Okay?"

"Yes, okay."

"Call us back as soon as you move the car. And stay in the car for now, okay?"

"Okay. Um, yeah."

"Okay. Bye for now."

"Um, bye."

He reached over and disconnected. Then he looked up at Michael. "Okay, Michael. You heard what I told her, that we'd get her to safety. Any ideas?"

"Well, yes, actually. We'll fly her out."

Phantom Air

"No, we can't risk putting her on a commercial airline, too many ways for them to track her." LaFleur took off his glasses and rubbed his eyes. "Jesus, this is getting crazy. This Lev character—I'm beginning to have very bad feelings about him. Ukrainian mob connections. Russian mob connections. Possible mob rivalries. And you heard what Karin said on the phone. Dirty bomb. And based on what we got off of Val's computer—sorry, you don't know about that—and you still don't. Like I told Blueray, 'plausible deniability.' It may be a cliché, straight out of a B movie, I know, but trust me on this. So, anyway, anything commercial is out. Plane, bus, train, rental car. Anything like that. Shit, Michael, I told her we'd get her out of there."

"And I told you, we'll fly her out."

"But I just said—"

"I know what you said. And I agree."

"Michael, what are you talking about? Tell me quick, I'm an old man and can't take much suspense."

"You're wearing that one out, A.C."

"Huh."

"Don't worry, A.C. I'm going to call Mother."

***

"I know this guy, an ace pilot," Michael explained. "Loves flying more than anything. Born to fly, not just a stick and rudder pilot, he knows airplanes inside and out—

engine, electronics, control systems, pressurization—he's checked out in more different aircraft than I can remember. He'd rather fly than eat. And—this is just icing on the cake—he has a brother in Big Timber, Montana, who's, well, sort of a survivalist type, but that stereotype is totally inappropriate for Pete. His place is perfect. He lives in this junkyard—"

"Ok, whoa, hold on. First of all, Mother?"

"Oh, yeah, guess that sounds strange. Uh, Mother is not his real name of course. Med school nick name. His real name is Matt Folker. We always called him Mother. Yeah, I know, but it was way before those movies. We always said they stole the idea from us. And we thought it was funny, at the time. We don't even think about it anymore, he's just Mother. He practiced medicine for awhile, but went crazy dealing with insurance companies—he's a real independent type—and so operated for awhile on a cash only basis, but that's almost impossible to do in upstate New York. So he finally just closed down his practice and spends all of his time flying."

"Okay. This Mother character, he's a crack pilot. And he has a brother in Montana." LaFleur paused, trying to sort out the wheat from the chaff. "And you're planning to get Karin to Montana, by plane, to Pete? Who lives in a junkyard? I'm not sure I like the sound of that."

"The junkyard is just cover; hasn't operated as a business for years. Pete has some great old stuff in there, though, in case he ever needs some quick cash. Pete's house is at the back of the junkyard, pretty much out of sight from the road. Great house. Looks a little rough from the outside, but inside it's all state-of-the-art. Even has a wine cellar; he's quite the connoisseur. But the real value of going to Pete is that he is really under the radar. He went dark years ago. Once we stash Karin with Pete, no one will be able to get to her until we say so. She'll be totally safe there."

"All right, I'll take your word for it. And you've already talked to Pete, he's okay with this?"

"Called him while I was waiting for you at the morgue. He's ready and waiting, just as soon as we get the details worked out at this end."

"And the pilot, Matt—sorry, Mother—do you think he's available on such short notice, for whatever it is you have in mind?"

"Sure, he lives to fly, like I said. I know he's in town. I talked with him the other day. He'd love to do it."

"We have time for this?"

"It's *all* we have time for."

"Call him."

***

After Michael got off the phone with Mother, they called Karin back to reassure her that things were in progress, not to worry, wait for the next call. It seemed to calm her somewhat.

"Mother is on the way to Watertown Airport," said Michael, as he and LaFleur walked to their cars. "We'll meet him there and he'll explain the details."

"He can really get her out of there without anyone knowing about it?"

"If he can't, no one can."

The phone rang. It was Karin.

"Karin. Have you moved the car? You're in an out of the way place?"

"Yes, Mr. LaFleur. Behind the Olympic Center, behind some trucks. They look like they've been parked here for awhile. I don't think anyone comes back here much. Is that okay?"

He would have preferred that she had moved out of town, but decided that given the circumstances, it was good enough. "Sure, that sounds perfect. We're on our way to the airport now; we're going to have someone fly up there to pick you up, okay?"

"Okay. Uh, soon? Because Fedir—"

"Yes, we understand, Fedir is on the way there. But he's at least two and a half hours away. We have plenty of time."

He said goodbye to Karin, once more reassuring her they'd get there before Fedir, and broke the connection. He turned to Michael. "How long does it take to get to Watertown?"

"Little over an hour," Michael replied.

LaFleur pondered that for a second. "In my car, sure. But in that hot rod of yours, shouldn't take more than forty-five minutes."

***

They pulled into Watertown airport forty-one minutes later. Michael had averaged a little over ninety miles per hour. The radar detector hadn't made a sound the whole way.

Mother looked nothing like what LaFleur expected, in spite of the flight suit. Instead of an older version of a Top Gun hot shot pilot, he looked like exactly what he was, a retired doctor. Tall, dark haired, balding, he looked more like James Taylor than Tom Cruise.

Shaking LaFleur's hand vigorously, Mother introduced himself. "Hi, Matt Folker. Glad to meet you, Detective." At LaFleur's nonplussed look, he laughed and said, "I don't go by 'Mother' outside of the old crew—they just don't want to let it go. But from what I hear from Michael, you probably belong in the 'inner circle' Call me Mother. "

"Sure thing," LaFleur said. "But I'll be careful not to use your full name too often. Hard to pronounce."

"Exactly."

"All right." LaFleur motioned to Michael. "He tells me you can get our, well, our subject, out of harm's way. How much has Michael told you about the situation?"

"Just enough to make me agree that you need to be very careful about moving her around. Here, come over to the table here and I'll lay out in more detail what I proposed to Michael a little while ago."

As they sat down at an old Formica table in the airport waiting room—*ah, Formica, LaFleur thought, they haven't made that in years*—Michael came over and joined them with coffee. Mother pulled out a piece of paper and laid it on the table, turning it so both Michael and LaFleur could see it.

"First," Mother began, "we're leaving from Watertown for two reasons—it's an untowered airport, and this is where my airplane is at the moment. From here, I'll go straight to Lake Placid, pick up Karin, and then head for Bradford."

"Bradford?"

"Bradford County Airport, Towanda. In Pennsylvania. That's where the jet is."

"Jet?" This was getting complicated.

"Yeah, here, look. I pick up Karin in my Cessna—I won't file a flight plan, it's VFR weather at the moment, great visibility, no weather to speak of, so no need to worry about going on instruments—and then we go to Bradford to pick up a long range aircraft. Cessna'd take days to get there, and weather in that direction is a bit iffy, so we need the jet. Then we just—"

LaFleur held up his hands. "Wait. You own a jet?" He was not used to feeling quite so uninformed. He felt as if he'd just walked into a movie half way through and didn't even know the title.

"Well, it's not my jet," Mother said, almost apologetically. "It's a Czech fighter/trainer, called an L-39 Albatros. Relatively short range, but very fast. It belongs to a friend of mine; he's a member of a flying team out of California. They're between air shows, and he happens to be in Bradford, visiting family. With his jet."

LaFleur took a sip of coffee, wincing at the taste of non-dairy creamer, and motioned to Mother. "Continue."

"Okay. Once we pick up the L-39, we head for Montana. I'll use a fake registration number. We'll need to stop for fuel, we have a range of about five hundred miles and it's over fifteen hundred nautical miles—seventeen hundred miles—to Montana. That reminds me—Michael, did you bring cash?"

Michael nodded. "Two thousand. That enough?"

"If not, I'll cover it and you can pay me back later," answered Mother. "Low interest rate."

Mother pointed back to the plan he'd sketched out and continued. "At fuel stops, we use transient parking; Karin will remain on board unless she needs to use the facilities, no need to have her wandering around causing unnecessary speculation. Once in Montana, we'll need to land at an airport big enough for the L-39. I propose Big Sky airport in Ennis. Runway's long enough, they have jet fuel, and if I stay below twelve thousand all the way, and if we don't need to go on instruments, we can avoid all the Class B/C areas, so no need to talk to anyone. And Ennis is out in the middle of nowhere. Wide open, mountains on either side, only a couple of houses near the airport. No one will notice us coming or going. From Ennis, Pete will take her the rest of the way in a small plane, taking off in the wrong direction, then correcting to head back to his place. He'll land on the road near the junkyard, stash Karin, then get his plane back to Big Timber airport."

"Pete has an airplane, too?" LaFleur was not surprised at the answer.

"Of course," said Mother. "How else can you get around in Montana? Anyway, after we transfer Karin to

Pete's Cessna and he takes her to his place, I take the jet on to CRQ in California."

"CRQ?" These pilots sure loved their codes.

"McClellan-Mt. Palomar airport. Carlsbad. That gets the L-39 back close to home base."

LaFleur leaned back in his chair and let out a long, slow breath. "Well, under normal circumstances, I'd think something this elaborate was overkill. But then when I think of Karin sitting up there alone, with Fedir Bondurenko on his way to her, well, it doesn't seem so extreme after all. Especially after learning more about old Uncle Lev. And they've killed—twice—and surely won't hesitate to kill a third time. So I hope this works."

"No question about it, A.C.," said Michael. "This will work." Michael pointed to Mother's sketch. "At the Lake Placid end," he asked, "how do we get to Karin?"

"The airport is just out of town, a mile or less," Mother answered. He turned to LaFleur. "Where is Karin now, exactly?"

"Right in the middle of town."

"Good, she can walk to the airport from there, no problem."

"Okay, let's do it." He picked up the phone and dialed Karin.

"Karin. Someone is on his way to get you. He'll be there in—" He glanced at Mother, questioning. Mother held up a finger and whispered, *one hour*. "About an hour," LaFleur continued. "You need to walk to the airport, leave your car where it is. The airport is less than a mile away, just south of town."

"Yes, I know where it is."

"Good. Go there. Don't dawdle." Mother raised his hand to get LaFleur's attention. "Hold on a second, Karin," LaFleur said, turning to Mother.

"Tell her there's a waiting room at the FBO—the Fixed Base Operator office" Mother said. "I'll come there to get her as soon as I land."

LaFleur nodded. "Karin, go to the waiting room at the airport office. Don't tell anyone any more than you have to. Say you're waiting for a scenic flight or something. The person picking you up, Moth—Matt—will explain everything once you are on your way. You are going to Montana, by the way."

There was silence at the other end.

"Karin? You okay?"

"Yes, I'm okay, Mr. LaFleur."

"Okay. I know things are moving pretty fast. Once you're safe we can go over everything that's happened, try to make sense of it, and then decide what to do next. Hopefully I'll have some answers soon."

"Um, Mr. LaFleur?"

"Yes?"

"There is one other thing. It's—" She broke off.

"What's is it, Karin?"

"My father's funeral. It's tomorrow." She spoke so softly LaFleur could barely hear her. "They killed him, too, didn't they?"

"It looks that way." He looked down and closed his eyes, grimacing. *Jesus, he'd forgotten all about the funeral.* After a moment he looked over at Michael, jaw set, a determined look on his face.

"I'll take care of it, Karin" he said. "I'll call Abruzzo's Funeral Home right away."

"Thank you."

"Try not to worry. We'll get you through this. Oh, one more thing, Karin."

"Yes?"

"Take the battery out of your phone as soon as we hang up. No more calls."

"But what if—"

"Hang on, let me check on something." He held his hand over the phone and turned to Mother. "How will we stay in touch with you?"

"I've got a 'burn' phone. Can't be intercepted."

LaFleur nodded, marveling at the thoroughness of this guy, and uncovered the phone. "No problem, Karin, we'll use a throw away phone that can't be tracked."

"Okay, I trust you."

"Thank you, Karin. We'll decide what to do next as soon as you are safe."

As they said goodbye and ended the call, LaFleur looked over at Michael, then back to Mother.

"Well, what are we waiting for?"

ETA Bradford PA 10:43AM

As she walked past the Swedish Hill Winery on Cascade Road, she thought of Michael; they'd done a tasting there that weekend. Forever ago.

The airport couldn't be far. She'd been walking very fast. Every time she heard a car coming up behind her, or saw one approach from the other direction, she ran off the edge of the highway and turned her back, sometimes nearly running into the bordering woods.

Fields opened up on the left ahead of her, and she spotted a sign displaying a stylized white airplane swooping down over a swath of forest green. Lake Placid Airport.

She almost ran down the road.

***

"Karin?" she heard someone say. She'd been sitting in the FBO staring down at her shoes, trying to forget why she was here. She jumped up and turned around to see a tall, good-looking man in a flight suit walking over to her.

"Hi. I'm Matt Folker. You can call me Mother. I understand you chartered a flight this morning?"

Ten minutes later they were in the air.

Mother leveled off at about six thousand feet, set the trim, and looked over at Karin. "We're heading for Bradford, Pennsylvania," Mother said.

"Sorry. What?"

He pointed to a small black knob on one side of her headset, two large, light green globes covering both ears. Karin reached up to adjust the volume. "And pull the mike a little closer to your mouth," Mother advised, "you're not coming through very well."

"Oh, okay," She pulled the adjustable mike up close to her lips. "Better?"

"Yes, perfect. I said, we're heading for Bradford County Airport in Pennsylvania. Sorry if I rushed you out of the office back there, but we're trying not to take anything for granted. Do you think you were followed?"

"No, I'm pretty sure no one knows where I am. I left the car in the parking lot behind the Olympic Center and went right to the airport. I hope Fedir doesn't find it."

"Not to worry. I'm sure we beat him out of here."

"Why are we going to Pennsylvania? I thought Mr. LaFleur said we were going to Montana."

"We are, but not in this. Too slow. We're going to switch to a faster plane for the rest of the trip. A jet, sort of like a fighter plane. Very fast."

Karin didn't know quite how to respond to that, so she just nodded.

"You're taking this all very well," Mother said.

"Not really. I guess I put up a good front."

Mother laughed.

"Sit back and try to relax. We'll be there in about an hour."

***

Well, he said it was "sort of like a fighter plane," Karin reminded herself, looking over at the L-39 Albatros that Mother had just pointed out to her. She couldn't quite believe they were actually going to fly in it. It looked exactly like a fighter plane: long, pointed nose, stubby wings with sleek pods at the wingtips, a clear canopy covering two seats, front and back. It looked very fast; just sitting on the runway, wheels angled back, it looked like it was already moving.

Mother had parked the Cessna and tied it down, telling Karin to stay in the cockpit until he came to get her. After a quick visit to the FBO, he came back out to get her.

"Okay," Mother said, opening her door and reaching in behind her to grab a helmet and flight suit. "Let's go to the office and get you suited up."

A few minutes later they were walking together to the Albatros. As Mother guided her up the side of the aircraft and showed her how to get into the rear seat, she had a sudden thought.

"Uh, there is no, um, lavatory in here, is there?" she said loudly, talking through the closed visor.

"No, no, there's not," laughed Mother. "But we're equipped with what we call a PRT."

Karin looked at him quizzically.

"Pilot Relief Tube," he said. "Even have a female adapter for it!"

She looked at him as if he had just told her she'd be standing on the wing like a barnstormer, all the way to Montana.

"Seriously, though," he said, in a reassuring tone, "we'll be making stops every three hours or so, and there will be an opportunity for you to use the facilities, if we're careful. Are you okay for now?"

She nodded, relieved.

"Still, in an emergency, just ask how to use the PRT."

"I'm sure I *won't* need it, thanks."

No Gold Medal For Fedir

Fedir sat in the parking lot of the Saranac Lake "Nice 'N Easy" Mobil station, clenching the steering wheel, knuckles stretched and blue-white. He needed gas.

Karin was gone.

He'd driven up and down every inch of Lake Placid after leaving the Olympic Cottages. He'd talked to the owner there, a stupid old man in a checkered shirt. Yes, there had been a young woman here last night, the old guy had said. No, she left suddenly. Think she went west, or maybe back into town, he couldn't say for sure, but he thought west. Yes, toward Lake Saranac, he was sure. Sorry I can't help you more, he'd said.

So Fedir had made one more circuit of Lake Placid, and then had gone on to Saranac Lake, checking every motel and lodge parking lot along the way.

He smacked the steering wheel with his fist, pulled out his phone, and called Val.

"*Khristos*, Fedir, can't you do anything right? You've looked everywhere?"

"Her car is gone. She could be anywhere by now. I don't know why she didn't wait. She thought it was Jimmy texting, so why didn't she wait? I don't understand; maybe she has talked to someone."

"Shit, Fedir. Lev will be furious."

"We do not tell Lev," Fedir said, darkly.

"Fedir, what the hell is wrong with you? Of course we have to tell Lev. It will all be okay, Fedir, just as soon as you find Karin."

"*Pah*," Fedir said, in perfect imitation of Lev. "Forget Karin. Too late."

"Fedir," Val said. "Just get up here. You're in Lake Placid now?"

"Saranac Lake, close by," Fedir said.

"Okay, Fedir. Meet me at Ben's Pub in Kingston, it is on, what, you know where it is, close to Princess Street. We'll go to Pavlo's, and then head straight for Toronto. How soon can you be here?"

Fedir looked at the GPS. "Three hours. Goodbye."

Fedir hung up before Val could complain again about losing Karin, and ignored his calls as he drove slowly away from Saranac Lake. He didn't notice the small plane arcing overhead, heading east before circling back to the west, from the direction of Lake Placid.

Stormy Weather

The drive back to Oswego from Watertown was uneventful; Michael kept it down to about ten percent over the speed limit.

Glancing at his watch for about the hundredth time, LaFleur tried to visualize where Mother would be by now. It was only about a hundred and twenty-five miles, he thought he'd heard Mother say. So, factoring in take-off and landing times, it should be less than an hour before he got to Karin. It would take her, oh, thirty minutes or so to walk to the airport from the center of Lake Placid, so she should have been there waiting for him.

He had also been trying to calculate where Fedir would be about now. The road to Lake Placid—basically Highway 3 to Saranac Lake, just up the road from Lake Placid itself—meandered around a lot. Even without traffic, it would take Fedir at least three hours to get there from Oswego, and that was pushing it. And he certainly wouldn't be driving an SL.

Plenty of time, he kept telling himself. *We've got plenty of time.*

Just as they were passing Selkirk Shores, Michael's phone finally rang. He thumbed the answer button on the steering wheel. It was Mother.

"Got her!"

***

LaFleur hardly slowed down as he walked past his

restaurant manager and headed up the stairs to his apartment.

"Hey, Boss. You're late!"

"Executive privilege, Frank," he called out over his shoulder. "Take care of things for me for awhile, will you? I'll be unavailable for a while. SCU."

Uh-oh, thought Big Frank. Something Came Up. Not usually a good thing, he'd learned.

"Sure thing, Boss." He heard LaFleur's door close upstairs, then went back to the kitchen.

After a quick call to Blueray, asking him to come over ASAP, LaFleur powered up his computer and began searching for more information on the Bondurenkos, especially Lev. He had a feeling that they were really up against it this time.

He'd called the funeral director, Emilio Abruzzo, on the way back from Watertown. He hadn't talked with Emilio since the investigation into Angie Frascati's death four years ago. Emilio had taken over for his dad, Enrico, sometime in the nineties, when Rico'd gotten too old to deal with the business. Enrico had been well aware of the details of Angie's death, as was Emilio, and under different circumstances it might have been easy for LaFleur to have become distracted by discussing old times. In this case the immediate need of rescheduling a funeral crowded out any other thoughts. It was, not surprisingly, something Emilio had never had to do before, but he assured LaFleur that he would take care of it.

LaFleur had moved on to researching possible nuclear threats that could be related to the plutonium Jimmy had texted Karin about. He'd just started on his third page of notes when Blueray knocked at his office door.

"Hey, kid, come on in," LaFleur said. "Thanks for coming over on short notice. Things have heated up again."

Blueray started to settle into a recliner in the corner. "Fill me in."

"Let's wait for Michael," LaFleur answered, checking the time. "He should be here in a few minutes. We need to do some serious brainstorming. Thunder and lightning, hurricane-level brainstorming. In the meantime, would you mind going down to the kitchen and asking Frank what he can get the kitchen to throw together for a late breakfast? Tell him I'm in the mood for blintzes."

"Sure thing, A.C." Blueray said, getting back up. "Back with breakfast shortly."

"Thanks."

Blueray turned, went back out into the hall, and bounded down the stairs. "Hey, Big Frank!" he hollered, calling to LaFleur's restaurant manager. "We need food up here!"

As Blueray made his way down to the restaurant, LaFleur pushed his chair back and looked up at the ceiling, as if he might spot the Cessna going by overhead.

"Hang in there, Karin."

Fedir Wants a Beer

As soon as Fedir got off the phone, Val immediately called Lev, who was, as Val had predicted, furious.

"God damn Fedir! Valentyn, why can't you take care of him?"

"Lev, you sent him by himself—"

"Yes, I know. Don't tell me what I did! Fedir, Fedir, Fedir! If only—no, never mind." He paused. "So, Valentyn, you do not know where maybe Karin has gone? You two were very close, yes? You know," he said, with warmth that surprised Val, "that is why I sent Fedir, not you."

"Lev, I don't know where she might be. I really don't." He was surprised by the catch in his voice. He had really liked Karin. It was a shame that it had come to this.

"Well, in any case, she knows too much. Too much. Listen, Valentyn, I will take care of Karin. I should have known—but no matter. I will make some calls, it will be done. We cannot let this stop us now, distract us. It is too bad it is more complicated, but it is no matter. You do not disagree?"

"No, Lev, of course not."

"Good. So, anyway, Valentyn; you take care of things now, everything is still set to go. You get Fedir, he is up there close to you somewhere, yes?"

"Yes, he is on his way here, to Kingston," Val said.

"Good. As soon as you are done there, you go to Odessa, yes?"

"Sure, Lev."

"Okay, you go now. You call me when you have Fedir,

when you are done at Pavlo's, and when you are finished in Odessa. Make this work, Valentyn. This has to work."

"Sure, Lev, we can do it."

"And Valentyn—"

"Yes, Lev?"

"Do not worry about Karin."

Val switched off the call.

Ah, Karin.

***

Lev called Vasily into the library.

"We need to find this Karin. You know what Fedir has done, yes? Chased her to Lake Placid, now she is not there. So. Here is where she is living." He handed Vasily a scrap of paper with the address of Karin's apartment in Oswego. "Go there; see what you can find out. Also, go to Valentyn's apartment, she was living there, I think, part time; search the apartment, see what you can find that might lead us to her. Anything.

"Let's see, then you go to Lake Placid, oh, and you also call our friend Anatoly and have him do his thing on the computer, the net, make his calls, whatever it is Anatoly does, his internet magic. You find this girl for me."

Vasily nodded and bowed out through the library door. Anatoly was there fifteen minutes later.

***

At just after noon, Fedir came in the door at Ben's Pub. He looked like death on toast—one of Jimmy's favorite expressions, Val remembered.

Ah, Jimmy.

"Sit down, Fedir. We don't have much time. And I called Lev, you know."

"Of course, I know you have to tell him." He sat down

and looked around for the waitress. "I need a beer."

"Sure, Fedir, one beer, and then we go. We've got to get over to Pavlo's. You follow me in your car; we'll leave it there when we go to Toronto."

"Yes, sure."

Val thought he'd better go over the plan with Fedir one more time. Fedir was so slow sometimes. Fortunately they were in a quiet corner booth; no one would overhear the conversation if they kept their voices low.

"You know what you are supposed to do, right?" Val asked.

"I have a backpack; we both have a pack, with some of the radioactive medicine. We use those to do a bomb scare. I go to my spot in Commerce Court; you go to stock building. Before you are coming back from there, I call 9-1-1, I have it written down, what to say, and then we go to the car."

"You call as soon as I start back to you, Fedir."

"Yes, that is what I said."

"Okay, Fedir. Tomorrow morning in Toronto we will go over again exactly where we will leave the packs. How we make the call. Everything. You remember how we practiced that before, right?"

"Yes, sure."

"Good. There can be no problems."

"But what about Karin? Lev said that—"

"She's gone now, and running, so she can't interfere. Lev will take care of it later. We have to concentrate on doing this job now, okay?"

Fedir nodded.

"Fedir, you have to get over this, this problem with Karin. Lev is mad now, but he is taking care of it. We just have to make sure this all goes as planned tomorrow. It is *very* important, Fedir. You can do this, yes?"

"Sure, Val. I can do it."

"Okay, then, let's go."

"But I never got a beer."

"You can have a beer in Toronto, Fedir. We can relax tonight. And after tomorrow, you can have all the beer you want."

***

"Pavlo. Let us in!" Val called through the door to Pavlo's apartment, banging on the door at the same time.

There was no response. "Pavlo! Pavlo, it's Val!" After again getting no answer, he turned the knob—it was unlocked, Pavlo was such an idiot—and forced the door partially open, catching on the chain lock.

"Pavlo, cousin! *Shcho z vamī?*"

There was scratching as the chain was removed. The door opened. Pavlo stood there, bleary-eyed.

"Nothing is wrong with me, Valentyn. I was just asleep."

Val and Fedir moved quickly into the apartment, closing the door behind them. "Come on, Pavlo, let's go," Val said, glancing around at the paraphernalia littering Pavlo's living room. "We need our stuff. The bag that was delivered to you."

"Yes, Valentyn, I have it for you. A moment." He went into the other room and returned a few seconds later carrying a zipped canvas bag. He handed it to Val.

"Uh. Heavy."

"Yes. Everything is there. Inside a lead bag."

"Ah, yes, of course." Val opened the top of the bag and glanced in. "Okay." He waited as Pavlo stood there looking at him.

"Pavlo."

"Yes, Valentyn?"

"The cross, Pavlo. Go get the cross."

Pavlo came back a minute later with the small box containing the golden cross and handed it to Val. "Take it away from here; I don't like to have it."

"No problem, Pavlo, you've done your part." He motioned to Fedir. "Fedir, give him your car keys. Pavlo, we are leaving Fedir's car here for a couple of days; park it in a safe place."

"Okay, Valentyn."

"Don't drive it while we are gone," said Fedir. "And park it away from a tree, I don't want it all messed up. And don't—"

"Come on, Fedir," Val said, "we're wasting time. We've got to get to Odessa, right now." He started out the door.

"Okay, Valentyn. And Pavlo, don't mess with the radio, either. I have it set—"

"Fedir!" Val yelled.

"Okay, okay! I'm coming!"

As he walked out the door, Fedir stopped and turned back. "Don't drive it, Pavlo!" he called.

"Fedir! Come on!"

"Okay, okay!"

"*Khristos*," Val muttered.

***

It was just after two when Val and Fedir arrived at the location they'd been given for the meeting with Semilovich. It was a large house sitting by itself at the end of a dirt road just outside of Odessa, hidden by trees, and protected by a creek on one side and a gravel pit on the other.

As they drove up and parked in front of the house, two men in dark suits stepped out of a large shed they had driven past, just at the edge of the driveway, and stepped behind the car. They stood shoulder to shoulder, blocking the exit. As Val opened the car door, two more men came out onto the front porch. One of the men motioned to Val to stay in the car as he walked towards him. Val slid back into the seat and closed the door quickly.

"*Khristos*, Fedir, these guys look serious." Neither Val nor Fedir had been to Semilovich's before; all of the negotiations to this point had been done by Vasily, as Lev's surrogate. Lev had not wanted to take the chance of anything going wrong before the stock plan was executed in Toronto, so had kept Val and Fedir insulated from the deal, until now. But now it was time for everything to go ahead. Lev was on a very tight schedule.

The man leaned over next to the car and waved his hand, indicating that Val should roll down the window. Val complied, and the man leaned in closer, holding up a picture to compare with Val's face. After a moment, he appeared satisfied, and motioned for Val to get out. As Val stepped out of the car, Fedir also opened his door, only to be warned by the man on the porch, "You stay." Fedir slipped back into the car and closed the door quietly behind him, unusually subdued. He nodded at the man, who pointedly ignored him.

Val pointed to the back seat of the car, and reluctant to speak, raised his eyebrows to ask permission to open the back door. The dark suit nodded agreement, and Val got the small box containing the cross out of the car. Holding it gingerly in front of him, he followed the man up onto the porch and into the house.

Once inside, he was told to sit in a chair by the door, while the box was taken from him.

"Wait," he was told.

Ten minutes later, the box was returned to him.

"Good," he was told, and directed to leave.

Back in the car, Val turned to Fedir. "Call Lev and tell him we passed the test."

They were afraid to look back as they drove away, and were soon on their way to Toronto.

Real-Time is Your Time

Blueray had just finished giving Big Frank the breakfast order. It had taken longer than Blueray expected, since he'd had to listen to Big Frank explain why he was leaving certain body parts to medical science—"my wife, she talks a lot, see, a whole lot, and I think they'll be interested in seeing the effect that has had on me; my eardrums are ossified, see, and my vocal chords nearly perfect, they never get used. See what I mean?"

LaFleur had met "Big Frank" Ivanovich at a veteran's benefit a few years earlier. There was no question as to why "Big Frank" was called that—he was big; really, really big. But not fat. LaFleur liked to describe Frank as being built like a six-foot four-inch tank, three hundred and fifty pounds of solid bouncer material.

They had discovered they were both descended from White Russian émigrés, in LaFleur's case on his mother's side; her name had also been Ivanovich.

Frank was a Viet Nam vet. He'd served as a medic, he'd originally told LaFleur, but then had started dropping dark hints about all sorts of other shadowy activities—working as a sniper for the CIA, for example. LaFleur brushed it off as good-natured bullshit. In any case, by the time LaFleur had driven Frank home they had become friends.

After Viet Nam, Big Frank had come home and gone to medical school on the government's dime, and had practiced as a "country doctor" in and around Oswego for years. But when he had decided to give up medicine, he'd suddenly found himself unoccupied. He hadn't realized how much he would miss the constant interaction with people he'd had in his practice. Managing the 1850 House restaurant gave him the opportunity to socialize a bit, and help out LaFleur.

Michael came in and rescued Blueray just as Big Frank was beginning to tell him about the time he'd—

"Sorry, Frank, need to talk to Michael." Frank looked around.

"Oh, Hi, Michael."

"Hi, Frank."

"Just ordered breakfast, Michael," Blueray said, heading Frank off. "Blintzes sound good to you?"

"Perfect. I'm ravenous. Had a long night."

"Didn't we all. I asked Frank here to make it a big order. We might be here awhile." Blueray motioned him to sit down. "We'll be right here, Frank, thanks a lot."

"Sure thing, kid."

Michael took a seat next to him and looked around. "Where's A.C.?"

"Upstairs. Thinking."

"Uh-oh. He throw you out?"

"No, no. He's waiting for you, actually. He wants us to come up as soon as breakfast is ready. He said you could help him narrow things down."

"Ah. He's in Occam's Razor mode."

"Exactly. 'The fewer assumptions you have to make to fit the facts, the better the chance your solution is correct.' Or, as he sometimes says, 'simpler is better.' Usually works. He's very good at it. Oh, I know he's old and a bit settled in his ways, but when it comes to sifting out the facts, he always gets it right in the end. He has some sort of innate ability, some way to eliminate all the irrelevant crap. It's amazing. I'm trying to figure out how to model it programmatically. If I can get it right, I'll be the next software billionaire you read about in Wired magazine."

Michael looked incredulous. "Billionaire? By emulating LaFleur?"

"Sure. I'm working on a program I'm calling 'Naked Truth.' It's an analytical tool based on an algorithm I'm developing that does what LaFleur does, just on a computer. I start with a mathematical formulation of Occam's Razor called Solomonoff's inductive inference, then use some set theory and a form of Bayesian analysis to factor in probability distributions, along with a standard Monte Carlo simulation. Then I add 'the LaFleur factor,' what I think of as his ability to differentiate between relevant and irrelevant data. It's devilishly hard to model."

"Okay, you lost me at 'mathematical formulation.' And 'Naked Truth?' Assuming that you can get it done, are you sure that's the best name for a program like that?"

"Well, that's just a working title. A lot of the best names are already taken. I'll come up with something."

Big Frank poked his head out of the kitchen and interrupted. "Got a big plate of blintzes ready to go. Made them myself."

Michael and Blueray stood up and walked to the kitchen door; Frank pushed through with a platter of food.

"Looks great, Frank, thanks," said Michael.

"So, what's going on?" Frank asked, as he handed over the platter. "A.C. still working on the jeweler thing?"

Michael nodded as Blueray took the platter and started towards the stairway. "Yeah. Things are starting to heat up."

"Well, let me know if I can help," Frank said. "I have contacts you know. CIA, NSA. Anything you need, you let me know. I'll make some calls."

Michael managed to keep a straight face. "Sure thing, Frank. We'll be sure to keep you in the loop."

"No trouble," Big Frank said. "Anytime."

***

"Big Frank says he'll contact the CIA for you if necessary, A.C.," said Michael, laughing, as he and Blueray rejoined LaFleur upstairs.

LaFleur looked up sharply. "Don't laugh," he said. "It's true."

Michael cocked his head in disbelief. "Are you kidding?"

"Nope. Frank's got connections. After the war he was deep inside the security community. Very deep. I may take him up on his offer if things turn sour."

"Well, okay," said Michael. "But he sure doesn't seem the type."

"Yeah, he's got quite an act. But now let's get back to business." Michael and Blueray settled into their respective chairs, plates balanced on their laps.

"Okay, now that we've got Karin safely on her way, we can get back to what we were doing—trying to figure out just what in hell the Bondurenkos are up to. This is what we know. What we think we know, so far, that is.

"Until Jimmy was killed, we didn't have much to go on. Never saw a motive for Armand's murder, and no real suspects. With Jimmy's involvement with Valentyn and Fedir—fatal involvement, as it turns out—we start to see a connection. The Ukrainians were using him as a sort of mule, taking radioactive materials across the border into Canada." He took a forkful of blueberry-cream cheese blintz and chewed thoughtfully.

Michael took this opportunity to go over to the corner of the room and turn on the TV, surfing until he found his favorite cable news station.

"What are you doing?" asked LaFleur. "Do we really need the television on?"

"Helps me think," replied Michael.

"Makes me go blank," said LaFleur.

"That too," admitted Michael. "I can't sleep without it."

"You can't sleep without UNN?" Universal Network News, a recent addition to cable news, was Michael's cable channel of choice. It bridged the gap between CNN and Fox, he claimed—no nut jobs on either side of the divide. LaFleur was withholding judgment on Michael's recommendation until he saw what UNN did with a celebrity murder case. That seemed to drive any news channel to hysteria.

"I sleep with the television on all night," said Michael. "A hold over from my resident and on-call days. Just ignore it. It's like white noise; it's soothing."

"Okay," said LaFleur, with a wave of the hand. "Anyway, where were we? Okay. None of this was making a lot of sense. Until we just happened to come by some interesting information on Val's computer—thanks to Karin and Blueray, we know at least part of what they have planned. I also called Larry, Arlene's husband—he's an economist—and he went over some of the data with me last night. So we have a pretty good idea of what they have planned; at least rough outline, if not the exact details.

"They were—are—going to plant radioactive materials somewhere in the PATH complex in order to cause a panic. The radioactive stuff they stole from the hospital—with Karin's key card, no less—is relatively harmless. Stuff used in diagnostics and radiation treatments, but low level, not all that dangerous. But radioactive enough to show up on a detector. So they plant this stuff, and then presumably call in a bomb threat. The authorities arrive, sure enough, the detectors start beeping, and before you know it there is a panic. News gets out, 'dirty bomb in PATH.' This causes a sort of 'flash crash' on the Toronto stock market—maybe a similar but smaller reaction on the New York exchange—and a large number of stocks that Lev & Co. have shorted fall in price, particularly those known to be held by Mendelokov. They snap them up, and cash in on the spread once the panic is over—it won't take the authorities long to determine that it is just low level contamination, nothing dire—and they are done. They don't want this to be a long lasting crisis. They just want it to last long enough for them to cash in their orders."

As LaFleur paused to chase an errant blueberry around the edge of his plate, Michael raised his hand. "This is what they killed Armand over? And Jimmy? Just taking some more or less harmless medical substances to Toronto, to fake a dirty bomb? Create some short term havoc, sure, and a chance to maybe make some money, not at all guaranteed. Is that enough to kill for? Twice?"

"Exactly. And that's what I thought, too. Though people do kill for the strangest reasons. 'Reasons' in quotation marks. But you're right; in this case it seemed obvious we were just missing something. Then we learned more from Jimmy. He texted Karin twice; once on his way back from Kingston, and once a while later. The first text was jumbled, and we misunderstood what he meant by 'hot jewelry,' and as a matter of fact, I don't think I had a chance to tell Karin what he might have meant by that—not that the jewelry was 'hot' as in 'stolen,' but actually hot. Temperature hot. As in plutonium 238. I found a reference on the web describing the chemical and physical properties of plutonium. That isotope—238—naturally gives off heat; that's why it's used as a power source for remote devices, like spacecraft." Blueray was nodding while LaFleur explained what he'd come to believe Jimmy had been trying to say.

"The next text," LaFleur continued, "the one she told us about this morning, made it even more explicit. Even though it was just a partial message. Probably still texting when they killed him." LaFleur grimaced at the thought. "Damn."

He shook his head slowly and continued. "So, what do we make of Jimmy's later warning, specifically saying they had plutonium, and mentioning a dirty bomb. Why plutonium? This is what really has me puzzled. They don't *need* the plutonium for their phony bomb scare. In fact, it could cause problems for them. As far as I see it, they want in and out of this radiation scare in PATH very quickly. The detection of plutonium among the materials they plant would cause a much bigger reaction than they want."

"Because the plutonium is so much more dangerous?" Michael asked. "That stuff is, what have I heard, the deadliest substance on the planet."

LaFleur shook his head. "Yes and no. Plutonium in itself is not all that toxic. It's an emitter of very low energy particles that don't really do a lot of short term damage, alpha and beta particles. You can stop alpha particles with a piece of paper. From what I understand, you could even eat plutonium without too much risk—it would just get flushed out of your system." Michael looked skeptical.

"But in any case," LaFleur said, "plutonium would certainly be cause for alarm, more so than some simple medical isotopes. If it's aerosolized and gets into the lungs there is considerable risk of long term damage, cancer.

"But that just doesn't fit this profile. They are not carrying out a true terrorist attack in the PATH complex. They just want the initial panic that *any* kind of radioactive incident creates. So I don't completely get the plutonium angle, not yet. Especially if it is plutonium 238 and not 239. And if it is 239? Completely different story. That could mean anything from a really nasty dirty bomb, even worse than 238—all the way to an actual nuclear device, a plutonium 'pit.'

"But I'm not sure we should make strong assumptions either way based on the somewhat incoherent nature of Jimmy's text messages. I think we *can* be reasonably sure that whatever they are doing beyond the PATH scare—which is only Phase One, so to speak—it involves plutonium, probably 238. So there is apparently a Phase Two, a secondary plan involving some form of plutonium that is *not* related to their stock market scheme. At least that's my thinking at the moment."

Michael's attention was suddenly co-opted by a news report on UNN. Television wasn't the total white noise generator he'd claimed it was, apparently.

"A.C. Look at this." He pointed to the television, reaching for the remote to turn up the volume at the same time.

They all turned to see a newscaster reading a special report—"Real-Time Is Your Time" as the channel would have it—concerning an upcoming G-8 summit to be held in Ottawa.

"—sources close to the situation say. The Royal Canadian Mounted Police have said only that they are working closely with agencies across Canada and the U.S.—including the CSIS, CIA, and DHS—to determine the validity of the threat. Again, as we just reported, sources close to the RCMP and the Canadian Security Intelligence Service say that credible reports of a threat to the G-8 summit to be held in Ottawa later this week have been intercepted. A source close to UNN, who insisted on anonymity, say the threat is possibly nuclear in nature, but would not elaborate. Again, sources say—"

"Jesus," interrupted LaFleur. "Talk about good timing."

Michael lowered the volume as the reporter continued to drone on with pointless observations and unconfirmed speculation. "As I was saying," LaFleur said, then stopped to look over at the television, watching the banner scroll across the bottom of the screen—*Nuclear terror threat—real or imagined?*—"as I was saying…plutonium."

This took a moment to sink in. Then LaFleur picked up where he'd left off.

"So, plutonium, certainly. But what variety? And what is Lev doing with it?" He turned to Blueray. "I think you can help out with that," he said, forking the last bit of blintz into his mouth. "We need to find out as much as we can about Lev's connections, his history, his recent movements. We need to nail down exactly who this character is and what he's been up to. I also want you to find out everything you can about any missing plutonium, whatever variety." Blueray stood up and moved his chair closer to the desk as LaFleur sat back and set down his empty plate.

"And while you are doing that," LaFleur said, "I'm think I'm going to call the F.B.I."

How to Make a Killing in the Market

While Fedir and Val were leaving Ben's Pub, on the way to meet Pavlo, Lev was sitting on his deck looking out over the lake. He was on the phone with Vasily. He was not happy.

"So, her car was parked in Lake Placid after all? And Fedir could not find it? Where was it? Okay, okay, never mind. And so she left Lake Placid in an airplane. What airplane? Okay, good, you got the number of the plane? Good, very good. So it won't be hard for Anatoly to track them, yes? Oh, you find it already."

After a moment, Lev held the phone away from his ear and looked at it, as if the phone itself could explain what he was hearing.

The airplane Karin was in, the airplane she left Lake Placid in, rather, the airplane with the registration number of the plane she left Lake Placid in, was sitting in a hanger in a tiny little airport in Utica, New York. Yes, the numbers matched; according to the log at the airport, it was the same registration number reported when the plane had taken off from Lake Placid. But as it turned out, the airplane in Utica had no engine and was covered in a thick layer of dust. It looked like it had not moved for years.

***

Vasily sat on the side of the desk opposite Lev, in the library. Anatoly sat next to him.

Anatoly was not quite as large as Vasily, but still muscular, and impeccably dressed in a dark business suit. His longish black hair was glossy and brushed back. He wore lightly tinted glasses with fancy titanium frames, indoors and out. Lev thought the glasses made him look like Las Vegas pit boss, which Anatoly thought was cool. Also, he couldn't really deny it.

Anatoly was to Lev what Blueray was to LaFleur. He was a graduate of both the famous Moscow technical university, MIPT—"Phystech"—and Harvard Business School. Lev had never been quite sure why Anatoly wanted to work for him. Whatever it was that had "radicalized" him, whatever had forced him out of the mainstream, Lev figured he was better off not knowing. All that mattered was that Anatoly was a computer genius, and had proven himself to be extremely loyal. And, after all, Lev paid very well.

The conversation over how to find Karin had just about run down. They'd explained to Lev that given the head start she had, finding her any time soon was a very long shot.

"In any case, she has run, maybe far away," concluded Lev, "and is very scared. This is good. This is maybe good enough for now. By the time she is brave enough to come back, we will be gone."

Lev paused, thinking of Val's involvement with her, and the fact that killing Karin would just complicate things even more. It was bad enough that they'd killed Jimmy and his father—and for nothing, really—so it was almost a relief to Lev that he could forget about Karin for the moment.

"Okay. Good." Lev slapped his hands face down in front of him on the desk. "Then we are done for now."

"Not quite, Lev," said Anatoly. "It concerns Karin."

"Yes? I thought we were done with her, she is run off, *pfft*, no worries. For now."

"There might be more to it, Lev. The airplane from Lake Placid, it reported the wrong registration number," Anatoly said. "Even so, I know where it landed."

"And?" asked Lev, impatiently.

"The destination was Bradford, Pennsylvania."

"So she may be there? Why did you not go there? Maybe we can still find her."

"That's the problem. Many airplanes leave from Bradford, every hour. She could have been on any of them. She could be anywhere."

"Yes, yes, this we already talked about. So?"

"So she could never do this on her own, Lev. This all points to a very complicated escape plan. She had help." He turned and looked at Vasily. "And if she had help like this, whoever helped her probably knows a lot about your, well—about certain recent activities. And maybe even more about what is planned. Someone knows, Lev. And we think we know who it is."

Lev lowered his head and glared at Anatoly, obviously not liking the sound of this. "Go on," he said.

"You remember that you asked us to check up on Dufresne, after Jimmy met with him, just to make sure nothing had gone wrong." Lev nodded. "We managed to find out that Dufresne had been visited by a detective—not from the Oswego police department, he said, but someone hired by Karin."

Lev shifted in his chair, visibly disturbed by what he was hearing.

"And we have to assume that Karin told this detective about Jimmy's last text, the one sent accidentally the night Jimmy was killed. And so," Anatoly went on, "it doesn't really matter if we find Karin or not. She has already told someone else."

"Yes?" Lev asked.

"Dufresne said it was a Detective LaFrance. But he had the name wrong."

Lev sat forward in his chair, grabbing the arm rests. "*So who is it?*"

"An ex-Oswego police detective named LaFleur."

Lev closed his eyes and then opened them slowly, turning to Vasily. "Take care of it," he said.

Vasily lightly patted a bulge in his coat pocket.

"No, Vasily," Lev cautioned. "Quietly, some kind of accident or something. We don't want to attract any more attention than is necessary." Vasily gave a quick nod.

"But soon. Take care of it soon."

Welcome to Pete's Place

So this is what an airport in the middle of nowhere looks like.

As the jet rolled down the runway and slowed to taxi speed, Karin couldn't help thinking about how utterly *remote* this place was. Upstate New York was certainly not an urban hotspot, and Oswego—well, at least Oswego had streets, houses, businesses, traffic lights, gas stations. Ennis Airport had—nothing. She had glimpsed the town of Ennis off to the northwest as they'd come in, but it flashed by pretty fast.

Once they came to a stop, Karin had a chance to look around and appreciate how beautiful the area really was. Lush, green meadows, ringed by blue and white mountains; dirt roads branching out in all directions, dead-ending, most of them, at the edge of the mountains. And yes, a truly big sky. She'd heard of that book, what was it? Of course, The Big Sky, by A.B. Guthrie. Pioneers. Indians. Mountain men. She'd have to look that up when she got home tonight. *Wait a minute, where am I?*

"Here's where I leave you, Karin," she heard Mother say, jolting her back to reality.

"Uh. Yes. Okay. This is where, um, Pete is picking me up?"

"Right. We won't have to wait very long; I called him as we were making our approach. He should be here in a few minutes. He was sitting on the runway at Big Timber waiting for my call."

"You guys work pretty fast. I still don't know what's happening to me."

"Yeah, it's been a real rodeo, that's for sure."

The small jet engine wound down quickly, and a few minutes later, Mother popped the canopy. "No one around, as you can see. You're safe to get out and stretch. Use the facilities, over there in that building on the left. But don't take long; we still want to get you wrapped up at Pete's as quickly as possible."

"Thanks. I'll be quick."

After Karin had climbed down onto the ground, she pulled off her helmet and handed it up. "Right. Won't be needing that in Pete's little 182," Mother said. "You probably won't be flying at an altitude any higher than about eight thousand feet from here to his place."

On her way back from the flight office, which had been deserted, Karin heard a small plane approaching. Mother pointed up at it and said, "Ah, yes, the happy sound of general aviation."

Fifteen minutes later, Karin had been introduced to Pete and was on her way to Big Timber. Wherever that was.

***

Pete, Karin was not all that surprised to learn, looked exactly like what she imagined one of A.B. Guthrie's mountain men to look like: short but extremely fit-looking, with a weather-beaten, reddish face, long white hair tied back in a ponytail, and a flourishing white handlebar mustache. And not one for much small talk, she'd quickly found. After a quick "glad t' meet ya," he exchanged a few words with Mother regarding the next stage of the plan, waited until Mother had reported in to LaFleur, and then Karin was off again, this time in Pete's little blue and white Cessna.

Slightly more than an hour later, they were on the ground again, landing on a dirt road, which Karin had been told would happen but had forgotten, and which had been the most frightening part of the trip so far—it was almost dark, and Karin couldn't even see where they were landing.

Once out of the Cessna, Pete quickly bundled her into an old Jeep Cherokee, which at first glance looked like complete junk, but had a clean, well-maintained interior, and ran perfectly. Karin could see that Pete was more concerned with substance than show.

Pete drove quickly back towards town, explaining to Karin that someone would be by in the morning to take the plane back to the airport. It was a regular thing, he said. She was quite prepared to believe that at this point.

Pete drove to the end of Mallard Springs Road and down into a small ravine, stopping near the banks of the Yellowstone River.

Karin looked around. They were sitting in the middle of a junk yard. Old cars everywhere. She thought she recognized a Studebaker Hawk. Or maybe it was a Packard, she wasn't sure. *Dad will know, he's an old car nut; I'll ask him later*, she thought. Then she remembered.

Just when she had started to feel safe.

"Let's get you inside," Pete said.

As Pete led her up the narrow path through the junk cars, she suddenly felt a great fatigue wash over her, and she almost stumbled. Pete's arm came out to steady her, and he led her up onto a large porch on the front of what appeared to be a small, but very solidly built log cabin.

As Pete ushered her through the door, he said, "Welcome to Pete's Place, your new home away from home."

Karin couldn't help but smile. But as she looked around, she became a bit disoriented. The great room they were standing in was at lease thirty feet long and nearly as wide. Karin looked back at the door they'd just come in, and then around the room again. She turned to Pete. "Am I Alice, and have I just fallen down the rabbit hole? This place didn't look very big from the outside."

"Ah," Pete replied. "Yes. It's built into the hillside, you see. I've got over three thousand square feet in here, with a façade that looks like a simple three room cabin. Very effective camouflage. It also has a survival shelter on a lower level: twelve hundred square feet, filtered ventilation, its own underground spring-fed water supply, and provisions for two for sixteen weeks."

"Wow, I guess I've come the right place."

"Indubitably," said Pete, face glowing with pride.

Karin laughed for the first time in a week.

Sharpening the Razor

LaFleur was still trying to find the number of his last known good contact at the F.B.I. when the phone rang. It was Mother. After a quick conversation he switched off the call and held up his hands. "Hey! Announcement!"

Michael and Blueray both turned toward LaFleur.

"Good news this time. She's at Pete's!"

A high-five from Blueray and a "Way to go, Mother!" from Michael concluded the short ceremony; the relief on all parts was evident.

LaFleur turned back to his phone list. "You'd think *one* of these guys would still be working," he groused.

An hour later, he gave up and asked Blueray to find him a number for the Royal Canadian Mounted Police.

"We don't have quite enough to call them yet, but I think we're closing in on it." He motioned them to slide their chairs over next to him. "Let's see if we've got anything solid," he began, "and if we all agree, we'll put in a call."

"Before we go much further, A.C., I've got something on plutonium that might be important," said Blueray.

"Shoot."

"There was an incident reported recently that could have been a source for illicit Plutonium 238," he began. "There's something called an RHU—Radioisotope Heater Unit—used primarily in spacecraft. You know, like the Mars rovers. Russian spacecraft use them, too. Anyway, a Russian scientist had twenty-four grams of plutonium 238 that he 'harvested' from a lab that was closing down, for

'for safe keeping,' he said. But he claims he couldn't get any government official to respond to his requests to pick it up. And then it disappeared.

"And twenty-four grams is *plenty* of plutonium, more than enough to cause the kind of trouble we're talking about," Blueray said. "After this news got out, a few days ago, government agencies everywhere have been falling all over themselves trying to locate it. Oh, and I should mention, the lab was part of the NSAU—the National Space Agency of Ukraine."

"Jesus, Joseph, and Mary!" exclaimed LaFleur. "Yeah, I'd say that 'might be important.' Okay," he said, making some quick notes on a yellow legal pad he had been holding. He looked up. "Got it.

"Now I'm going to lay out a couple of different cases for you," he said, "then you tell me what you think. Most of this will be familiar—we talked about a lot of it earlier—but I just want to go over it again in a summary manner." Michael recognized this technique from the previous cases he'd been involved with—LaFleur liked to organize everything in a straightforward, logical manner, and then—as Blueray had emphasized earlier—apply his own unique version of Occam's Razor. "Let's continue to call this first case 'Phase One,' just to keep things straight.

"One: Lev and the boys—damn, just a second." He reached over to his desk and grabbed a pair of reading glasses. After putting them on and adjusting them on his nose, he began again. "Okay. Lev and the boys have been trafficking in radioactive materials. Two: some of the materials are relatively benign, of no obvious use to anyone outside of a hospital. Three: information was acquired from Valentyn Bondurenko's laptop"—he nodded subtly in Blueray's direction—"that included financial and stock trading account data and detailed layouts of the Toronto PATH system. Names, dates, places.

"My conclusions: there is a high potential for some sort of diversion, some kind of disruptive incident, to be staged in the Toronto PATH complex, the intent of which is to manipulate the market in such a way as to profit on a flash crash of sorts—that is, cause a short term drop in prices in order to cash in on a large number of short sales. The stocks involved point to Lev's former association with a known Ukrainian mobster; both profit and revenge seem to be motives."

"The radioisotopes from the hospital," Michael said. "That stuff really isn't all that, well, radioactive, is it? And it decays quickly. That could cause a panic?"

"I think the key is in the way they make the threat. You're right, those materials are only mildly radioactive, so they wouldn't just plant them and hope they somehow get detected. They must also be planning to actually call in a bomb threat, making sure they call out the fact that it is a 'dirty bomb.' Once that is established, even the weakly radioactive materials they plant would be easily detected by first responders—they'd be looking for them—and it would not be initially obvious how highly radioactive or potentially dangerous the bomb might be. Everyone is primed for a major event. It would be a case of assuming the worst. That could very easily start a panic."

He looked up from the legal pad, raising his eyebrows in anticipation of any objections. "Any other comments?"

"Nope. I think you've nailed it, A.C.," was Michael's response.

"I agree," said Blueray. "Based on what you saw on Val's computer, I think the links are solid."

"Okay," said LaFleur. "It's actionable. Blueray, that number for RCMP, think that's the right division?"

"Best I can do. I think they'll at least understand what you're talking about."

"Let's see what they say." LaFleur said, reaching for the phone.

***

"Well, I've had more pleasant conversations with my proctologist" said LaFleur, as he switched off the phone. "That guy reminded me a little of Dudley Do-right. Though I have to admit, even to myself I would have sounded a little unhinged. It is a pretty crazy scheme I described to him."

"But did he take it seriously?" asked Michael.

"Hard to tell, but I think near the end he was convinced I wasn't a complete nut case. He'll enter an incident report; hopefully that will make its way up the channels. But it's obviously not enough. The files on Val's laptop all point to tomorrow as D-Day. We're really coming in under the wire here. Ideas?"

There was a studied silence.

"Come on, guys. We're not here on vacation."

Blueray shifted forward in his chair. "If we're sure of our data—"

"We are."

"And we trust your conclusions—"

"I do," said Michael.

"Then we need to make sure we've got it covered, even if the RCMP doesn't come through."

"I can tell by the fire in your eyes that you've got an idea, Blueray."

"Well, A.C., it involves one of your pet peeves."

"There are so many to choose from, I can't begin," said LaFleur.

"Social media," answered Blueray.

"What, we put out a terrorist alert on Facebook?" asked LaFleur, jokingly. Michael chuckled. He knew what LaFleur thought of most modern social media networks.

"You know me better than that," retorted Blueray. "Listen, if someone can hack the AP to cause havoc—

remember the Twitter rumor that caused a split-second market crash last year? Well, why can't we—okay, I—infiltrate a few reputable sources to plant a story that is actually going to *prevent* an incident?"

"Tell me more."

"Think of it as a sort of crowd-sourcing. Or better yet, as Warren Buffet's concept of the market as a voting machine. Wait a sec." He held up his tablet and started swiping across the screen. Twenty seconds later, he held it up for Michael and LaFleur, pointing to a highlighted phrase in a document. "Here, this from one of Warren's essays." He read it out to them: "He says, 'In the short run, the market is a voting machine but in the long run it is a weighing machine.' We're dealing with the short term here. So we don't have to worry about the 'weighing,' the long term aspect. We focus on the ability of the market to behave in the short term on a kind of immediate 'majority rule' basis, rather than relying on long term analysis or historical weightings. We just need to make sure the market understands that there is no real threat."

"You're losing me," said Michael.

"No. I get it," said LaFleur. "If we sufficiently advertise that fact that the threat is bogus, and make it appear that the consensus is 'there is no real threat,' then we have counteracted any adverse affect that threat might have. We can defuse it, real-time. Just post the truth, on as many reputable outlets as we can."

"Exactly!" exclaimed Blueray. "So you *have* been listening!"

"I try," said LaFleur.

"So, how do we pull this off?" asked Michael.

"The timing is crucial," replied LaFleur. "Too soon, we look like we're the ones trying to disrupt the market, too late and the panic sets in and they have succeeded. How sure are we of the date, the time?" He looked at Blueray. "Can you pinpoint a definite target?"

"Like we said, tomorrow is fairly certain; as to time; well, they'll want to time it such that the crash takes place early enough for them to see the bounce, and take advantage of it, but late enough that the market closes soon after. Nothing is certain, but if this was a bet in this year's World Poker Tournament at the Rio, I'd go all in on two P.M., tomorrow."

"Set it up."

***

A little later, Big Frank brought up lunch: pulled pork sandwiches, coleslaw, his special recipe cowboy beans, all washed down by Saranac Legacy IPA. While they ate, Michael turned the television volume up a bit and they listened again to the news on the security alert. There was nothing new.

It took some effort to renew their focus after a good lunch, especially given the meager amount of sleep they'd all had, but LaFleur insisted they move on to what he called "Phase Two."

"So, what do we make of the plutonium?" he asked, after downing the last of his Saranac. "One: We know Jimmy took over a small amount, probably about two grams, based on what he told Karin. Two: he specifically warned Karin about a 'dirty bomb,' or some other terrorist action utilizing the plutonium. Karin's initial information was very sketchy, but in a later brief conversation—as she was being spirited away—she confirmed what Jimmy had texted, or attempted to text, right before he was killed. Three: We've lost track of Val completely, and all we know of Fedir is that he was on Karin's tail last time we heard from him. Four: A major international summit is scheduled to take place in Ottawa next week."

He paused and looked around to see if there was more beer. There was. He opened a bottle and took a long draw.

"Five: Blueray has informed us of at least one possible, maybe even probable, source of black market plutonium 238 floating around out there somewhere.

"And concerning number one," he amended, "regarding Jimmy's role in transporting the stuff. They were using Armand's custom's pre-clearances to move it through as part of a routine shipment of scrap gold jewelry. In itself, not much to worry about. But—"

Michael interrupted LaFleur with a question. "A.C.? Aren't there radiation detectors at all of the border crossings?"

"Not as many crossings have radiation detectors as you might think," LaFleur said. "Mostly only major cargo ports. In that part of Canada, Montreal, certainly, and many ports in the U.S.; but it's not exactly well advertised as to whether there are detectors in place or not. But most likely nothing at Thousand Islands Bridge, where they've been crossing."

"And you said that plutonium is pretty easily shielded."

"Right. So I don't think moving it would be a big problem. Of course, now that Lev doesn't have Jimmy, he'll need to adjust his game plan, but I don't think it's a deal breaker."

"I understand. Please, go on, sorry."

"Not at all. We need to consider every aspect of this, not make too many assumptions." He looked back down at the legal pad. "So, in my estimation, the one or two grams of plutonium 238 that Jimmy delivered must simply have been a demonstration of Lev's ability to move highly radioactive materials into Canada. But the inescapable *conclusion* I've come to is: there is more where that came from. And it may already be on its way.

"And I'll be damned if I know how to stop it."

This Doesn't Look Like a Motel 6

"Exit here." Fedir was studying the map and reading the directions they'd gotten off the hotel website, while Val tried to follow the navigation system, but he couldn't understand anything either one said.

"Sherbourne?" Val asked. "That doesn't sound right."

"Oh, yeah. I mean, no. Next exit after that. Yonge Street." *Yong-gay Strit.*

"I think it is pronounced 'young street,' Fedir."

"Okay, '*yung strit.*' I don't care. Next exit."

"Okay," Val said, exiting the Gardiner Expressway, "I'm on Young Street. What next?"

"It says, 'turn left on Melinda Street.' Then go into parking garage."

Val drove slowly down Yonge until he saw Melinda, turned left, and then, just as Fedir said, there was the entrance to the parking garage.

"Okay, Fedir, we're here."

Val pulled into the valet parking lane and stopped the car. The attendant came over as Val opened the door and got out.

"Good evening, sir. Welcome to One King West. May I call a porter?"

"Uh, no, uh, thanks. We can get it." He leaned into the car. "Fedir! Get the bags out of the trunk."

Fedir looked over at the valet, then at the hotel entrance. "Why are we stopping here?"

"This is our hotel. Just get the bags, okay?"

Fedir got the bags out of the trunk and followed Val into the hotel, as the valet attendant drove off. Once inside, Fedir looked around the lobby in amazement: marble floors, chandeliers, modern art, cozy little nooks next to gas fireplaces.

He followed Val to reception, not saying a word. But as they headed to the elevator after Val had checked into their suite, Fedir leaned close to Val.

"*Khristos*, Valentyn. A suite? And look at this place. We can't afford to stay here. Even Lev can't afford this."

"Shit, Fedir, by this time tomorrow afternoon we can afford to *live* here."

Road Trip

After another hour and a half on the phone with the RCMP, LaFleur pushed his chair back in relief.

"Well, it took awhile, but I finally worked my way to the correct division, a National Security Enforcement Section." He checked his notes. "They have quite an operation. These NSES offices fall under the, uh, let's see, the NCSI: National Security Criminal Investigations. And under each NSES, they have teams, INSETs: Integrated National Security Enforcement teams. These guys are specialists, inter-agency, not just RCMP. Work with U.S. agencies, too, but I'm not sure we're going to get that level of cooperation. Anyway, I convinced them I'm not a nut case and they want to meet, first thing tomorrow morning. We're scheduled to meet with an Inspector, a pretty high rank if I understand it correctly; Inspector Mallory."

"Wow," said Michael. "So that means…?"

"That means, Toronto! That car of yours gassed up?"

"Yeah," Michael replied. "Ready to go when you are."

"Good." He swiveled his chair in Blueray's direction. "Blueray, you have the web thing ready to go, your internet news feeds, whatever it is you're doing?"

"Almost ready to go, A.C., I need about an hour to finish coding; then it's just a matter of entering a couple of simple commands, and the scripts do the rest. We'll be flooding the net with information countering the bomb scare. It's sort of a crap shoot, since on the net you never know what is going to take and what isn't, but I think we have a good shot at it. I've also set up feeds into the major news organizations; hopefully they'll run with it. With you on the agency side, along with the information we float out there, we might be able to attract enough attention to counteract anything the Bondurenkos try."

"Good enough. I'm going to leave you in charge here—well, you'll be reporting in to Newton, of course," he said, as the cat came into the room and jumped up onto the desk—"while Michael and I do what we can at that end."

"Got it. That okay with you, Newton?" Blueray asked.

At the sound of his name, Newton turned to Blueray and blinked slowly, as if to say, *whatever*.

"Make us a reservation at a hotel in downtown Toronto, Blueray. As close to a major PATH access point as you can, preferably near the financial district. Yeah, I know" he said, waving away a concerned look on Blueray's face, "it might be expensive. But we need to try to be within spitting distance of wherever the Ukrainians attempt to pull off their little charade." He stood up.

"Michael, how far is it to Toronto?"

"Oh. I don't know, two hundred and some, probably two hundred and fifty miles?"

"Say two-fifty. That's what, four hours?"

Michael gazed up at the ceiling, calculating. "I think I can do it in three."

"Okay! That's what I like, initiative!" He started for the door. "Go get packed; I'll let Maggie and Frank know what's going on. Meet you downstairs in an hour."

"Okay. I'll call you when I get here; I'll park in back."

"Perfect. See you soon."

Michael headed downstairs while LaFleur went into the bedroom to throw some things together. Then he called Maggie—she was volunteering at the hospital that afternoon. She'd be right home, she said.

In the meantime, LaFleur went down to the restaurant to explain things to Big Frank.

"Frank, a big SCU."

"Not surprised. What is it?"

"I've got to run up to Toronto with Michael. We're pretty sure we know what the Bondurenkos have going on up there, and we're going to try to stop it."

"I take it the investigation into the jeweler has expanded a skosh."

"You could say that. Look, I know I can trust you to be discrete—we think there's going to be a dirty bomb scare staged in Toronto tomorrow afternoon. Blueray has an idea about how to counter it by putting the real story out on the net. At the same time, I'm going to try to convince the RCMP to take the threat seriously. So, yeah, it's gotten complicated, and this could just be the beginning of something even worse. And we're still a long way from actually determining how and why Armand—and his son, Jimmy—were killed."

"If I can help—"

"You'll be the first person I ask."

***

The shadows along East Bridge Street were stretching in the lowering sun; couples meandered in the park across the street from the 1850 House, enjoying the late afternoon calm.

Maggie and Frank walked out with LaFleur, Frank walking ahead and carrying LaFleur's overnight bag, Maggie hanging on LaFleur's arm. Blueray had made a reservation for them at a hotel close to the Toronto-Dominion Center, in the center of the business and banking district. Michael had called from the parking lot behind the restaurant a few minutes earlier.

"Call me as soon as you get there," Maggie said as they turned the corner on Fourth and walked down the street to the lot.

"Don't worry," LaFleur replied. "We'll stay in close contact."

Frank had reached the lot ahead of them and was walking to Michael's car; Maggie was still holding LaFleur's arm as they reached the wide driveway, LaFleur on the outside, near the street.

He heard it before he saw it; the sound of a car accelerating through the intersection behind them, and a short, sharp squeal of tires on pavement. Out of the corner of his eye as he turned his head away, LaFleur saw a large, black car swerve into the oncoming lane, coming north from the opposite side of Bridge. He instinctively pushed Maggie away from him, toward the building, and began to turn away himself just as the car came up over the curb and onto the sidewalk. He grunted in pain as the left front tire of the car smashed his right foot. With another screech of the tires, the car jerked away to the right. He fell.

Frank, up ahead, heard a short scream—Maggie—and then a thud and a loud "*oomph*" as LaFleur hit the ground. He turned just in time to see a late model BMW sedan swerve back over into the right lane and speed off down Fourth.

"Sonofabitch!" hollered LaFleur, reaching down and grabbing his right foot, rolling back and forth in pain. "Sonofabitch!"

Frank ran over to him and bent down. "You all right?"

"Shit, no!" yelled LaFleur. "Ran over my goddam foot!"

Maggie knelt down beside him and cradled his foot in her hands. Michael had just realized something was wrong and came up to them.

"What happened?"

"Goddam car ran me down!" said LaFleur. "Frank, did you see it?"

"Sure thing, A.C., it was a BMW, black, 5-series, late model, probably '12 or '13. New York plate LMG-something, couldn't make out the whole thing."

"499," said Maggie. "I didn't get the letters, but the numbers were 499." She gently lifted LaFleur's foot up off of the ground. "I'm going to try to take off your shoe," she warned LaFleur. "Let me know if it's too painful." She unlaced his shoe—he still wore old-style black dress shoes, Florsheim cap-toe, a true detective shoe. As Maggie loosened the tongue and started to slip it off, LaFleur grunted in distress.

"It might be broken," she said. "We should get you to the hospital."

"Hell, I don't have time for this," groused LaFleur. He reached down and helped Maggie ease his shoe off. She carefully probed along the instep and the arch. "Yow! Don't do that again!"

Maggie shook her head. "I think you have fractured metatarsals. You've got to get this treated."

LaFleur looked up at Michael. "Ah, hell, it's probably not any worse than a stubbed toe. Michael, what do you have that you can give me to block the pain? A local anesthetic, something that won't mess me up."

"I'm not sure that's a good idea, A.C.—"

"Maggie, you get me one of those boots, what d'ya call 'em?"

"Orthopedic boot?" asked Maggie.

"Yeah, that will immobilize it, right? And Michael, you can deaden it, just for now. I'll get looked into after we're done in Toronto. You can do that, right?"

"I suppose lidocaine or bupivacaine would do it," said Michael. "They're commonly used in hand and foot surgeries."

"Perfect. You and Maggie go to the hospital, Michael, get the drugs you need, Maggie, grab one of those boots, then come back and get me.

"Frank, help me back upstairs. Let's see if we can find those bastards!"

***

Frank and Blueray were sitting in front of LaFleur's computer discussing how to go about tracking the hit-and-run. LaFleur sat on the couch, foot propped up, nursing the Scotch he'd used to wash down a few ibuprofens. He hoped Michael got back with the needle soon.

"Blueray, can you hack the New York DMV database?" asked LaFleur. "Get a name, address?"

"I don't like to use the word 'hack,' A.C., I 'infiltrate;' get in and out without notice," said Blueray.

"I stand corrected. Can you *infiltrate* the DMV? That could give us the owner. 'LMG' is an Oswego county plate."

"Possibly," said Blueray.

"But from what you guys have been telling me," interjected Frank, "these guys aren't going to be stupid about car registrations. It could be a wild goose chase."

"Good point," said LaFleur, "but we've got nothing to lose, right? Can you do it, Blueray?"

"Sure. Well, I think so." He pulled his chair up closer to the computer and reached out for the keyboard.

"I'd like to know where that car is right now," said Frank.

"And where it's been," said LaFleur. "Can we do that, too?"

"If we're lucky," answered Frank, "that car will have a tracker installed, like LoJack, or one from the manufacturer. Once we have the VIN, we can worm our way into *those* databases. They used this trick a lot at the agency. It was practically a required course at The Farm."

"Frank! Loose lips!" LaFleur called from the couch.

Frank laughed. "Do I look like Edward Snowden to you? This stuff is well known, A.C."

"To you, maybe. I'm just a small town cop. Small town *ex*-cop." He looked over at the open office door. "Ah. I think I hear Maggie and Michael. About time!"

Maggie went to the couch and carefully fit the orthopedic boot over LaFleur's foot.

"Don't put too much weight on it," she warned. "We don't' know the extent of the injury."

"Don't worry," LaFleur replied. "Couldn't if I wanted to." He winced as Maggie tightened up the straps on the boot. "What a botched job. Think that crowd would be a little more professional."

Maggie looked up in disbelief. "You are the only person I know who would complain about *not* being killed."

"Well, you know what I mean. But it indicates to me that they are getting desperate, rushing things. Which means our guess as to the timing of their plot tomorrow, and whatever else they have in mind following that, is probably good. We don't have much time."

Maggie handed him a cane. "Okay, try to get up and walk. Let's see if you're up to chasing Ukrainian terrorists all over Canada."

He stood up and tentatively put the broken foot down.

"*Ow*. Sonofabitch, that hurts. They should'a just killed me."

"Knock it off, or they won't have to," said Maggie. But she was smiling as she said it.

Toronto: One King West

"This is a very nice bar, Valentyn."

"Yes, Fedir, it is."

They had been sitting at Henri's, in the lobby of One King West, for about four hours. Neither one of them had any idea of how large a tab they'd managed to run up. It was extensive.

"Those pork sliders were very good, Valentyn."

"Yes, Fedir, they were."

Fedir raised his glass, a Bombay Sapphire gin gimlet. He'd never had one before. "Tomorrow, Valentyn."

"Yes, Fedir, tomorrow!"

They looked around. It was quiet, a week night. No large corporate meetings going on, none of the regular Saturday night hook-ups being arranged, no bachelorette parties with their singing and dancing and lewd gag gifts scattered all over the bar tables.

"Well, Fedir, I think we had better go up now. 'Call it a night,' they say."

"What is that, '*call* it a night?' That makes no sense. What else would you call it, Valentyn? It *is* night."

"Never mind, Fedir. Come on, let's go. We have important work to do tomorrow. I want to get a good night's sleep, and not rush. We have to do a good job, Fedir."

"Okay, yes. Maybe one more Bombay?"

"No, Fedir. I still want to make sure nothing goes wrong."

Val motioned to the bartender, a pretty young girl; she hardly looks old enough to be in here, he thought.

"I will pay for the bar bill, okay?" he asked.

"Certainly, sir. One moment." She turned and walked to the bar computer and came back a minute later with a bill. "Please sign here, with your name and room number. Any time you're ready," she said, walking back to the bar.

Valentyn looked blankly at the bill. He remembered the room number, but was not sure what name he'd used to check in. He motioned the waitress back over to the table. "I can pay in cash, yes?" he asked.

"Of course, sir."

Val pulled out his wallet and carefully counted out the correct amount, rounding up slightly, but only about two dollars, just to make it come out even; someone had told him that you were not supposed to tip in Canada. The look the waitress gave him made him wonder if that was true.

"Come on, Fedir. Let's go."

***

The drive up to Toronto had been the longest three hours LaFleur could remember. His foot hurt like hell. Michael said it was not a good idea to keep the foot numb for long periods of time, but he agreed to deaden it again tomorrow when they had to go out.

When they'd left Oswego, Big Frank and Blueray had still been working the hit-and-run ID. As a higher priority, LaFleur also had them working on the plutonium angle. They promised to call, no matter the time, as soon as they had anything new.

LaFleur lowered himself into a lobby chair as Michael went to reception to check in. He looked around.

Christ, Blueray, he thought, *I know I said not to worry about expense, but still...*

Marble floors, chandeliers. He looked over at the bar, just visible from where he was sitting. Henri's. Looked very nice. He could use a Famous Grouse.

Michael came back over and interrupted his reverie.

"Okay, we're set. Here, give me your bag." He took LaFleur's travel bag, and then leaned over to help him up.

"Using a cane a little sooner than I'd planned," LaFleur said.

"We'll get you taken care of properly as soon as we get back to Oswego," said Michael. "This way to the elevator." LaFleur followed him out of the lobby, hobbling in his boot, trying to figure out how to use the cane effectively without tripping over it.

The elevator door opened and they stepped in. Michael pressed the button for their floor. Just as the doors were closing, two rather inebriated men rushed up and stepped in at the last minute.

"Thanks," said one of the men.

"Sure," said LaFleur. "What floor?"

"Um, nine," one of them said.

LaFleur pushed nine. He and Michael were on four.

The elevator stopped at four, and LaFleur and Michael stepped out into the hall. Without thinking about it, LaFleur glanced back over his shoulder and casually said "good night," an unconscious pleasantry.

"*Na dobranich*," said one of the men, the obviously drunker of the two. The other man looked out at them. "Good night," he said, "he means to say just 'good night,' that is all." He said this with a heavy accent. The elevator doors closed.

LaFleur turned to Michael.

"Jesus Christ, Michael. Did you hear that?"

"You don't think—"

"Sonofabitch, Michael. We're in the same bloody hotel."

Toronto: PATH

Once they were settled in the room, LaFleur and Michael made a plan, of sorts. Since they didn't know exactly when the Bondurenkos were going to launch their "attack," they couldn't give the authorities an exact time, or much warning in the event. They arranged for Blueray to be ready to launch his online "counterattack" at any time after one P.M, though they expected it to be closer to two or maybe three.

Blueray had provided them with headsets for their phones. He said that would be more reliable, and more importantly less conspicuous, than two-way radios. LaFleur agreed; you saw people walking around everywhere these days apparently talking to themselves.

The broken foot added a complication—LaFleur would not be able to move as quickly as they expected the Bondurenkos to be moving tomorrow. The best they could do was plan for LaFleur to go out ahead of Michael, sometime after one. Michael would stake out the elevator in the lobby and warn LaFleur when he saw the Bondurenkos leave the hotel. Since the main King Street subway entrance was right in front of the hotel, they assumed that's the way they would exit; that entrance led directly to the Commerce Center shopping complex below ground, right behind the subway station.

They planned to go out together first thing in the morning to become familiar with the layout of the PATH complex near the hotel. LaFleur also wanted to locate the main financial institutions in the area above ground, in case they made any of those a target—the Toronto Stock Exchange itself, for example, which was only a long block away—so he had some hope of finding his way around the next day. Downtown Toronto, they'd already seen, was not easy to navigate; all the glass and steel started to look the same after a few blocks. The PATH complex could be even more confusing, even given the helpful directional signs: "you are in Hudson's Bay Company; North to Eaton Centre."

After a last check-in with Blueray, and a goodnight call to Maggie from LaFleur, they went to bed and tried to sleep.

***

The meeting LaFleur had arranged with the NSES took place at a nondescript building near the airport, just a few minutes away from the hotel.

RCMP Inspector Mallory, as LaFleur had sensed on the phone, was thoughtful, serious, and nothing at all like Dudley Do-right. LaFleur was impressed. More important, Mallory seemed genuinely impressed with the information LaFleur presented. The narrative LaFleur laid out—the murders, the isotope thefts, the plutonium fragments Jimmy had smuggled—was convincing, particularly in the context of recent events. Mallory had been making notes at his computer throughout the meeting.

"Well, Mr. LaFleur, you have a compelling case," Mallory said, indicating the meeting was concluding. "On such short notice, however, and based only on your admittedly thin evidence," Mallory continued, "I cannot at this time commit a large response." LaFleur began to object, preparing to make his case more strongly, but Mallory waved him down. "But, as I said, Mr. LaFleur, your case is compelling. To that end, I have authorized the participation of a small INSET team. The team will be available immediately." He reached over to a printer at the side of his desk, then handed LaFleur a single sheet of paper.

"Here are the details. Staff Sergeant Patterson in the outer office will make all the arrangements."

***

"I can't tell you how glad I am we'll have some backup," LaFleur told Michael as they parked the car back at One King West. "That Sergeant Patterson is all over this thing. Even if we've only got four officers, that's an army compared to just the two of us."

"I have to say I feel a hell of a lot better about it," said Michael.

"I'm a little surprised they are letting us go ahead with our little plan," LaFleur admitted. "But like Mallory said at one point, we know what and who we are dealing with. I guess they are content to just keep watch over us."

Michael parked the car and they started to walk through the garage to the hotel, but LaFleur stopped at the entrance.

"Listen," he said, "we don't have much time. I don't need anything back at the room at the moment. Let's get started."

Michael understood this to mean the reconnaissance of PATH and the surrounding area they'd discussed the night before. They had decided they'd begin at the point they presumed the Bondurenkos would be starting from later that day, the King Street subway entrance.

"I'll meet you back here in one hour," LaFleur told Michael, as they made their way down the subway steps.

"Don't get lost," Michael said.

"With this foot, I can't get far," LaFleur replied.

By eleven o'clock, LaFleur was back at the hotel lobby. Michael came in a few minutes later.

"Good timing," said LaFleur. "We have just enough time for a bite to eat. Then it's show time."

***

It was about two-thirty when Michael saw them coming out of the elevator. He immediately called LaFleur, who was waiting patiently at the west end of the Commerce Court shopping area, near the food court. Well, not so patiently the past hour or so, actually. He'd started to wonder if they had the timing right, and the anesthetic Michael had injected into his foot earlier was already starting to wear off.

"They've left the hotel," Michael said, as soon as LaFleur picked up. "I'm right behind them."

LaFleur. "All right, I'm calling in the reinforcements. Be back soon. You call Blueray."

"Right away."

Blueray answered just as Michael was following Val and Fedir out into the street.

"Hit the button, Blueray."

"The truth is out there," said Blueray a few seconds later. "News of the hoax will start appearing all over the place in a few minutes."

"Perfect, Blueray. Talk to you soon."

In the meantime, LaFleur scrolled to the number Sergeant Patterson had given him. They were standing discretely by, waiting for his call. As soon as he'd given Patterson the word that they were on the move, he called Michael back.

"Okay, I'll stay on line from now on. Patterson's team is in position, shadowing us. Does Blueray have "Operation Pravda" underway?"

"Yeah. 'The Truth is Out There,' in his words."

LaFleur chuckled at the X Files reference; just like Blueray. "Great. Okay, where are the Bondurenkos?"

"They've just gone down the stairway on this side of the street," said Michael, "into the King Street subway entrance. I'm right behind them. They are both carrying small, green backpacks."

"Okay, got it. I'm right in front of the food court; I'll be watching the entrance from the subway tunnel."

"Right." A few seconds later he updated LaFleur. "Okay, they are heading to Commerce Court, right in front of me."

"Got it."

"Okay. They just left the tunnel. You should see them any second."

"Yeah, there they are, heading this way."

"Okay. Fedir is turning right, now, you see him?"

"Yeah."

"Looks like he is heading down the passage towards Scotia Plaza. I'll follow him. Val kept going straight; no, now he's veering off to the right towards the bank."

"I see him. I'm on my way."

Michael saw LaFleur hobbling as quickly as he could down the passage behind Val. "Okay. Fedir is stopping near the end of this hall, looks like there is a stairway there, across from a flower shop. He's just hanging out there. Must be waiting for word from Val. You still see him?"

"Yeah. He's turning the corner at the CIBC bank, going left now. Ah. Heading into the TD tunnel."

"Did you say 'TD,' as in Toronto Dominion?"

"Yeah. Fortunately he's not moving too fast, just a casual walking pace. So far I can keep up okay."

"Okay. Fedir's still just hanging around."

"Okay. We're heading straight past the TD pavilion, I think. Hang on a minute." There was a break in LaFleur's progress report, but Michael could still hear him panting a little as he made his way down the passageway.

"Okay, Michael, still there?"

"Yeah."

"All right. Val just made a turn to the right, at the North Tower; wait, now a left turn—okay, let me check the sign. Yeah, he is heading toward the Standard Life Center. Anything change at your end?"

"Nothing so far. Just hanging around."

"Okay. We are in the Standard Life Center somewhere, uh, veering right. Hang on." Michael heard LaFleur's heavy breathing and an occasional snatch of conversation as other pedestrians passed. "Okay. Another right. We are almost—uh, wait; looks like he is heading up. Hold on." Michael could hear LaFleur struggling to keep up, and then heard traffic noise as he apparently got up to street level.

"I'm back up on King Street," said LaFleur. "Jesus, we're right across from the Stock Exchange Building. I thought he might be heading here. Yeah, he's crossing the street. Wait a minute."

LaFleur watched as Val walked across King and stopped in front of the Exchange Building. Then he saw Val turn around and stare at something back in LaFleur's direction. Val just stood there, transfixed, staring.

Christ, LaFleur thought, *did he make me? No, he's never seen me before. What the—?*

LaFleur turned in the direction of Val's gaze and looked up. "I'll be damned," he said.

"What is it, A.C.?" Michael asked.

"I'm watching the Reuter's news ticker above the entrance to the Standard Life Building. And would you believe it, Michael?"

"What?" Michael asked, urgently this time.

"The news, Michael, just the news. 'PATH bomb hoax exposed,' it says. There's more: 'Fake dirty bomb scare allegedly staged by two Ukrainian nationals. No cause for alarm, officials say. More on www.reutersnews.com.' Blueray, you're a genius!"

He looked back across the street and saw Val pull out a cell phone and begin speak into it frantically. "Hey,

Michael!" he said. "Did you just see Fedir answer his phone?"

"Yeah. He stepped back into the stairwell, and then ran back this direction. He's headed into the tunnel."

LaFleur watched as Val began to run back across the street, heading for the PATH entrance he'd left just minutes before. LaFleur stepped back behind a large sign as he passed. "Okay. It looks like Val has bolted; they're probably going to meet up at the hotel. I'm calling in the Mounties!"

He quickly called Sergeant Patterson and described what was happening. Patterson said they were already closing in; they'd been tracking everything.

LaFleur called Michael back. "Michael, Patterson's team is closing in now. I'm on my way back, but it's slow going. Are you at the hotel yet?"

"Almost there, A.C., just coming out of the tunnel at the King Street entrance."

"See anything?"

"Nope, no one in sight."

LaFleur had a sudden thought. "Try the parking garage. They may be trying to slip out that way."

"On my way."

LaFleur heard a shift in the background noise and street sounds as soon as Michael entered the underground garage, followed by the sound of screeching tires, car doors slamming, and confused shouting. "Michael, what's happening?" he shouted, causing a few heads to turn as he ran—hobbled quickly—into Commerce Court.

"They've got them!" Michael shouted back.

"Damn! I missed it!"

"Don't worry—I got it all on video on my iPhone!"

***

The debriefing took place in the same room where Michael and LaFleur had met with the RCMP the day before. It had only been an hour since Val and Fedir had been picked up in the hotel parking garage.

Both Inspector Mallory and Sergeant Patterson were present, as well as representatives from the RCMP Organized Crime and National Security divisions. Mallory had also asked an expert in radiological security from the Canadian Nuclear Safety Commission to sit in.

After the introductions were complete, and Mallory had brought everyone up to date on the current status of the Bondurenkos, he apologized to LaFleur for having initially doubted his story.

"Understandable," said LaFleur graciously, an affable swagger in his voice. "You were all working at a huge disadvantage. I'd been gathering information on those two for several days, and with assistance provided by Karin Broussard, along with some inspired web investigation"—carefully avoiding the words "hack" or "infiltration," Michael noticed—"by two associates, and certain files obtained by—well, let's just say we were in possession of all the data required. It was just a matter of the correct application of the principle of Occam's Razor to the data in hand."

"Occam's Razor?" asked Mallory.

"Ah, yes, let me explain," said LaFleur. Michael rolled his eyes, knowing what was coming.

"It's a methodology developed by a fourteenth century philosopher named William of Ockham, *o, c, k, h, a, m*—the modern spelling is *o, c, c, a, m*—which in its simplest form states that the hypothesis requiring the fewest assumptions which still explains all the available facts is the most likely to be correct. In this case I simply had to—"

"Well, that's very interesting, Mr. LaFleur," interrupted Mallory, "and we are in your debt. But now we must turn to the much less interesting, bureaucratic portion of our meeting. If you'll please take a look at the documents we've prepared, let's see, yes, we'll start with Mr. McFarlane of Security." He turned to the National Security representative. "Doug? Please begin."

LaFleur raised his hand, cutting off McFarlane before he could get started. "Sorry to butt in, but I still have unfinished business. Another result of our application of Occam's Razor to the available data, in fact." He paused while the room looked on expectantly.

"I haven't had a chance to tell anyone about the plutonium yet," he said.

A stunned silence descended on the room, as Michael would describe it later. LaFleur claimed to have actually heard a gasp of surprise, but Michael would not confirm this.

"Plutonium?" blurted the radiation specialist. "Plutonium?" he repeated, settling back down into his chair from the raised position he had taken at hearing LaFleur's statement.

"Um, yes," LaFleur said. "Lev Bondurenko—Valentyn and Fedir's uncle—he lives in Pulaski—has arranged to sell a rather significant amount of plutonium 238, as much as twenty or more grams, to a Ukrainian mobster named Arkady Semilovich. Exactly what Semilovich plans to do with it, we don't know for sure. But based on the timeline, and on current events, and on your own intelligence, it's likely that it is destined to be used in an attack on the G-8 summit to be held in Ottawa next week."

"But we've searched the car," exclaimed Mallory, "and the packs they were carrying have been rigorously inspected. There was no plutonium."

"Well, I'd search the boys' hotel room at One King West right away if I were you," said LaFleur. "Ninth floor. You'll find a hollow golden cross containing approximately two grams of plutonium 238. And as I said, there is more where that came from, and we know where it was going."

***

Mallory stopped LaFleur at the door as the meeting broke up—to be rescheduled as soon as necessary. "Mr. LaFleur," he said, "I have a question."

"Shoot."

"How on earth did this Occam's Razor theory of yours tell you where to find Valentyn and Fedir?"

"Oh, it didn't help at all."

Mallory raised his eyebrows quizzically.

"Oh, no," said LaFleur. "We just happened to bump into them in the hotel elevator. We stayed there last night, too."

Don't Shoot! I'm Wined To The Hilt

It had been forty-eight hours since the Bondurenko brothers had been picked up in Toronto. With Val and Fedir now in secure lockdown in the Millhaven Supermax prison in Bath, Ontario, Semilovich in high security custody in Toronto, and Lev apparently on the run, it was probably safe for Karin to come home.

The trouble was, Pete wasn't answering his phone.

Mother had tried several times to contact Pete using the safe contact phone, which inexplicably resulted in a "no longer in service" message. Michael also tried the number he had for Pete, with not even that result—it just kept ringing.

After another day of trying to get through to him, it became clear that Pete was *incommunicado*.

"Looks like Pete has veered a little off plan," said Michael, as he hung up the phone.

"Plan, hell," groused LaFleur. "He's apparently left the planet and is heading for Pluto."

They got on a plane to Bozeman the next morning, LaFleur in a jet splint and on crutches, grumbling all the way.

***

"Where do we go from here?" LaFleur asked, as Michael drove out of the rental lot at the Bozeman Yellowstone Airport.

"Big Timber," replied Michael, "about an hour from here. Over that way," he said, waving his hand in a generally eastern direction. "Just off of I-90, about half way to Billings. Pete's not actually in Big Timber, of course," he went on, "but close enough."

Almost exactly an hour later, Michael drove down the road at the end of Mallard Springs, and stopped at the edge of the junkyard. The path to the house was not immediately obvious—it took them a minute or two to spot the break in the tall weeds lining the road. Once on the path, they could see, however, that Pete didn't let weeds grow up around his car collection.

"This way," said Michael.

LaFleur followed behind slowly on his crutches. The X-rays had shown only minor metatarsal fractures, which allowed LaFleur to use the crutches in a "partial weight bearing" mode—he could stand putting some weight on the foot, but not much. It still hurt like hell, and the day running around in Toronto hadn't helped.

As they made their way along the path, LaFleur noticed that a few of the cars were in much better condition than he would have expected for a junkyard. There were plenty of rusted out old hulks, most not even good parts material, but scattered in among the hulks were what looked like very restorable classics. Pete had obviously been very selective about what he brought in here. LaFleur passed by what looked like an Auburn Boattail Speedster, weathered but intact, the open cockpit covered with a tarp. *There could be a fortune sitting out here*, LaFleur mused, as he looked around at some of the other vehicles.

They turned a corner about half way up the path and the front of the house came into view. At first it looked fairly conventional—a large log structure, with a huge deck in front, and two massive log pillars on each side of the front entry. LaFleur noticed something odd about the way it sat against the hill, and then realized that the back of the house actually disappeared *into* the hillside. *Looks pretty damn secure*, he thought. *Good choice.*

"When's the last time you were here?" LaFleur asked, as they continued up the path.

"Oh, at least five—"

Michael was cut off by the sound of a gunshot.

"Jaysus, what the hell?" LaFleur hollered, as they both instinctively ducked and backed down the trail several feet.

Michael knelt down at the side of the path, behind the Auburn. LaFleur crouched down beside him, leg sticking out awkwardly as he shifted his weight.

"Damn it! What the hell has gotten into him?" Michael said.

"Has he ever done anything like this before?" asked LaFleur.

"Well, not exactly," Michael started to say, and then caught himself. "Sort of. There was a situation a few years ago regarding a business license, Pete holed up and gave the county a hell of a time for awhile, when they tried to get him to acquiesce to a new fee or something to do with the junkyard. But nothing like this."

"Let's see if he's cooled off. Holler up at him."

Michael stood up and slowly edged forward, just around the side of the Auburn. "Pete!" he yelled. "It's me, Michael. I'm with Detective La—"

Another shot; Pete was still firing into the air as far as they could tell, but this time the shot was followed by a warning blasted out through a loudspeaker.

"Don't come any closer."

"Pete! We're here to—" Michael yelled, only to be cut off again.

"This is your last warning. Clear out, now!"

They cleared out.

Standing by their rental car a minute later, both catching their breath, LaFleur asked, "What now?"

"I have an idea," said Michael.

***

A little over two hours later, after a trip to Bozeman to visit a hardware store and a certain wine distributor Michael knew of, they were back at Pete's.

"No, this will work, I know it," said Michael, for about the tenth time.

"You're crazy," said LaFleur, for about the eleventh time.

"Just help me get these attached."

Michael stood by the car, arms outstretched, a roll of duct tape in his hand. At his feet were four bottles of wine. Very special wine, according to Michael. "Tape one bottle to each of my arms," Michael said, handing the duct tape to LaFleur. "Label forward. Then tape the other two bottles to my chest the same way, label forward, with the top of the label showing. He has to see the top of the label."

"Okay, but I still think—"

"This will work."

It took some long strips of duct tape looped under the bottles and around the back of his neck, forming sort of a harness, to hold the bottles in place on Michael's chest, but they finally got them secured. "Okay. You stay behind me," Michael said, as he walked back up the path to Pete's.

"Don't worry."

As soon as Michael cleared the Auburn, the expected warning shot was fired, followed by another loudspeaker warning.

"Don't come any closer. Last warning!"

"Pete!" Michael yelled up the hill. "Get your binoculars and take a good look at what I have strapped to my body. I think you will recognize it. Look closely." There was silence as Pete apparently pondered this development.

"Pete! Take a look. It's four bottles of Le Grand Vin de Chateau Latour. Look closely, Pete. You should be able to make out the castle tower on the label."

LaFleur hissed behind him, "*You're crazy.*"

"*Be quiet*," Michael hissed back. "Pete! If I fall, four bottles of Chateau Latour are going to go into the dirt with me." He waited another moment. There were no gunshots, and no loud warnings.

Michael took a cautious step forward. "Take a close look, Pete." One more step forward. "And Pete? They're vintage 1961!"

This time the voice through the speaker sounded calmer, inquisitive rather than threatening.

"Latour? 1961?"

"That's right, Pete."

"Michael? It's really you?"

"Who else would know which wine to hold hostage? Come on, Pete. Let us in. We're here for Karin."

LaFleur had edged up behind Michael. They both stood there, waiting for an answer.

"Okay," they finally heard Pete say. "Come on up. Slowly."

"Okay, Pete. We're coming up."

They were only about twenty-five yards from the house when Pete's voice came back over the loudspeaker.

"Hold it!"

They stopped in their tracks.

"What is it now, Pete?" Michael yelled.

"I get to keep the wine, right?"

Doctor's Corner, Revisited

The gathering in Doctor's Corner the night after Karin got back to Oswego was at once both celebratory and subdued. Four of them—Karin, LaFleur, Michael, and Maggie—were all struggling, in different ways, to make sense of the events that had taken place after that first meeting with Karin, just a couple of weeks ago. A fifth party present, Blueray, had not been at that meeting, but once LaFleur had brought him into the investigation, he'd proven indispensable; he'd earned his place at the table. As had the sixth, Big Frank. In fact, LaFleur gave him most of the credit for bringing down Semilovich.

LaFleur's initial goal at that first meeting with Karin had been simply to provide Karin some measure of support in the face of the seeming indifference of the police. He'd hoped for some measure of justice, of course, although his hopes on that front had been less optimistic than, say, Maggie's. Now, after the events in Toronto, there was no doubt they had been successful.

Karin had nothing but praise for LaFleur and Michael—for the way LaFleur had identified the killers, and the way Michael had arranged for her safe transit to Montana. She also couldn't praise Blueray and Big Frank enough for the technical expertise they'd shown in figuring out what Val and Fedir were up to, not to mention being responsible for the inspired internet infiltration that had brought them down.

And not only that, she stressed, but also identifying the location of Lev's buyer, Semilovich, and stopping the sale of plutonium. The RCMP had descended on Semilovich's compound within two hours of LaFleur's intelligence.

"You should have seen him, Maggie" Michael said, "explaining Occam's Razor to the Canadian feds. It was classic LaFleur. They didn't know what hit them."

"C'mon, Michael, it wasn't like that at all. All I said was—"

Michael, Blueray, and Big Frank all started hooting at the same time.

"Okay, okay," said LaFleur, grinning. "Maybe I lay it on a bit, sometimes."

After the noise died down, Karin asked, "How on earth did you track that car to Odessa, anyway?" Karin asked.

"Blueray? How did you do it?" asked LaFleur, waving in Blueray's direction.

"Well," Blueray replied, "it wasn't just me. Big Frank here had much more to do with that. He's the one who suggested looking for a tracking signal, like LoJack. As it turns out, that car hadn't been equipped with LoJack, but that didn't stop Big Frank. He was able to find data captured from the BMW Assist package installed in the car—don't ask me how, I think it's an NSA thing, but Frank isn't talking; those systems use GSM cell networks—to determine that it had been in Odessa four times in just the prior two weeks. So we figured that had to be the location. And sure enough, the RCMP quickly located Semilovich holed up there. They'd been looking for him for weeks." Frank beamed with pride. "And now Lev's sidekick Vasily is in jail for hit and run, too," Blueray said, "again, thanks to Frank."

"It's called 'vehicular assault' in New York law," said LaFleur. "And I hope they nail the bastard to the wall." He held up his foot.

Overall, they had all managed to keep the dinner conversation fairly light, even while talking about some of the more exciting aspects of the case, and as a result had they'd been able to relax and enjoy themselves. They had especially enjoyed hearing details of Karin's time in Pete's care.

"You just wouldn't believe the wine cellar," she said to Maggie at one point.

"That's for sure," agreed Michael. "We helped Pete store the bottles of Latour. It was amazing. He must have more stashed away in wine than in antique cars."

"And he's an excellent cook," Karin continued, "or should I say, 'chef.' He prepared some of the best meals I've ever had."

But as the desserts and after-dinner drinks were served, the mood became a bit more somber.

"I know I should be happy that Fedir—and Val—are in jail and will be for a long time," said Karin, "but I also can't help feeling that it's, well, useless, somehow. Oh, I know," she continued, anticipating objections, "they won't be able to do any more damage for a long time. And you—all of you—prevented a major catastrophe. If Lev had managed to deliver the plutonium…Well, yes, obviously there's no question that they are better off in jail. I don't know what I'm saying."

"I know exactly what you mean, Karin," said LaFleur. "Incarceration certainly has its uses, as in this case. Of course, we still don't know when the Canadians are going to release them for trial in the U.S., for the murders. They've got a very tight hold on them at the moment. I'm sure we'll get our chance, but it may be awhile.

"And of course, we don't have any idea where Lev is; no one does. Every three-letter agency in the northern hemisphere is looking for him, and the rest of the plutonium. Semilovich very cleverly never held any of it, and might even slip the net, again. He's nearly as untouchable as Mendelokov, it seems. So while we were able to stop the imminent threat, this time, unfortunately there could be a next time. So let's hope they find it, or Lev, or both. Soon."

"Val and Fedir—they haven't said anything that might lead to Lev?" asked Karin.

"According to Mallory, Val and Fedir have been talking their heads off, trying to make a deal of some kind. So it's very possible they'll provide a lead." He hesitated before going on. "There's one thing we learned—well, I don't know quite how to tell you this, Karin, but it seems that they used Jimmy in more ways than we suspected."

"What do you mean, Mr. LaFleur?" Karin asked.

"Well, we know now that their initial reason for breaking in to the jewelry shop was just to get the travel and customs documents they needed to transport the stuff across the border. And apparently they had some idea of planting the cross containing the plutonium sample in the scrap gold delivery, and then somehow intercepting it at the other end, at Dufresne's. Not a very good plan, which I think they soon realized. That's one reason they enlisted Jimmy to make the delivery. But there's one thing we never understood, and that's how they could have broken into your father's shop without setting off the alarm. It turns out that Jimmy inadvertently gave them the alarm code; as you know, it was your mother's birth date. Jimmy apparently let that little piece of information slip at some point, and it was a simple matter for Val to find the date."

Karin sat in stunned silence for a moment, staring down at the table. "So both murders were simply a result of being in the wrong place at the wrong time."

"More or less," agreed LaFleur. "You father, as we suspected, interrupted a burglary, though not related to the jewelry business in the usual sense. And Jimmy, well, he just got himself in too deep, I guess you could say. And then unfortunately brought you into it."

"But to change the subject, Karin," LaFleur went on in a lighter tone, "you mentioned earlier that you intend to go back to Montana soon? We never had a chance to hear the rest of that plan. You're closing down the business, I presume."

"Yeah, there's no way I can carry on with Dad's store. Especially not without Jimmy, even though he never—" She broke off and started over. "Anyway, I've lined up a position at a Deaconess Hospital clinic in Bozeman. Well, the clinic is actually located at the health center in Belgrade, just down the road, but it will be perfect. Day shift, no on-call, no weekends, usually, so I'll be able to spend a lot of time at Pete's—"

"Whoa!" LaFleur cried. "You and Pete?!"

"Now, Mr. LaFleur, don't jump to conclusions. Pete and I became very close, even in the short time I spent with him, and, well, he needs someone to—well, to 'socialize' him a bit."

Michael couldn't help but comment. "Wait until Mother hears about this!" he said.

At this point, Big Frank raised his hand. "I have a question," he said, pointing at LaFleur.

"What is it, Frank?" LaFleur asked.

"It's about this Occam's Razor thing."

"Yeah, go on," said LaFleur.

"Well, if you are so smart, and this Occam's Razor technique is so good, well, then…what's your prediction for what's going to happen between Karin and Pete?"

LaFleur was momentarily speechless. But only momentarily.

"Well, Frank, when it comes to the combination of red wine and romance, there's no razor sharp enough."

Karin and Maggie thought they'd die laughing.

Epilogue: Do I Know You?

It was almost closing time. Several weeks after the events in Toronto, LaFleur was glad to be back to a normal, dull routine.

LaFleur was just about to turn out the lights in the bar and lock up the restaurant. As he reached for the light switch, he heard the front door open, followed by the scraping of a chair. He grabbed his crutches and made his way out into the dining room.

A short, heavyset man was sitting in Doctor's Corner.

"Good evening," LaFleur said, walking up to the table.

"Good evening, Mr. LaFleur," the man said.

"Excuse me, but do I know you?" LaFleur asked.

"Not exactly," the man replied, in a strong accent that LaFleur found oddly familiar.

LaFleur raised his eyebrows, bemused. "We're about to close, I'm afraid, so we've stopped serving dinner," he said.

"Maybe just a drink, then."

"Sure. What can I get you?"

"A shot of vodka, perhaps?" asked the man. "Then I will go."

"Sure. Just be a minute." LaFleur turned to go.

"Please join me," the man said. "My treat."

LaFleur didn't quite know what to make of this. "Okay, sure," he said, after a moment.

"Wonderful."

LaFleur went back to the bar and poured out two shots of Stoli, then brought them out, carrying both in his left hand, using his crutch with the right. "Here you go," he said, carefully setting one shot down on the table.

"Thank you." The man picked up the drink and raised it to LaFleur. "*Na zdorov'ya*," he said. As the man raised his glass, LaFleur's eye caught a glint of a gold ring on one of the man's fingers.

"Cheers," LaFleur said. They tipped back their glasses and drank down the shots in one gulp.

"I have heard that you are a very good detective, Mr. LaFleur," the man said. "I could not resist the opportunity to see you. Just to tell you that…well, yes, just to tell you." He put down his glass, then reached into an inside coat pocket and brought out a heavy black leather wallet. He extracted a ten dollar bill and laid it carefully on the table.

"Thank you, Mr. LaFleur," he said. He stood up and picked up his hat, tipping it in LaFleur's direction before putting it on. "We will meet another time," he said, turning toward the door. He blinked slowly, heavy-lidded and serene. "Yes. There will be…another time. Perhaps *soon*." As he tipped his hat a second time, LaFleur got a good look at the ring he had glimpsed earlier. It was a large gold signet ring, with the visage of a lion carved into the face.

That looks familiar, LaFleur thought.

The man went quickly to the door and walked out.

LaFleur limped over to the door, but by the time he got out onto the sidewalk, there was no one in sight. He turned and went back in, locking the door behind him, and made his way back to the bar. He paused, took one more look around, and then walked over to the stairway to the apartment.

He suddenly remembered where he'd seen that lion before, just as he switched off the light.

Acknowledgements

As always, we want to thank all the friends and family who have helped us throughout the entire process of writing the book; without their continual support, encouragement, and engagement, we never could have done it, again.

As in the past, we've had invaluable assistance from several key contributors. Sarah Massey-Warren graciously reviewed nearly every chapter as it was written, saving us from many embarrassments; Kurt "Chicken" Schmitt, Noel Yantos, and Thomas "The Tree" Fountain provided crucial elements of the flight segments, along with many other excellent suggestions; Willie McLaughlin presided over a productive brainstorming session at the Copper Bar in Big Sky, ably assisted by Katrine Mahon; and a special thanks goes to Pete "Danger" Huisveld for his fine review comments and plot suggestions, and for being such a good sport. Additional ideas were provided by Arthur Handley, Rich Fiese, and Eric "Big Frank" Johnsen. We are also indebted to Detective Robert Latulip for his past help and inspiration.

Many valuable suggestions, along with editing and proofreading, were provided by a dedicated group of reviewers: Sandy Fountain, Adrienne Abbott, Bob Notorangelo, Nancy Margolis, Linda Lovold, Charity Fechter, and Debbie Abbott. Many thanks to all.

Any errors, of course, are ours alone.

Once again, we cannot give enough thanks to Bill Reilly and Mindy Ostrow for their continued support and unequaled professional advice, and for providing a wonderful outlet for our books: the river's end bookstore at 19 West Bridge Street, Oswego, New York, http://www.riversendbookstore.com.

About the Authors

Dr. John Fountain, after graduating from Wayne State University School of Medicine in Detroit, Michigan, traveled overseas to do his initial residencies, first spending two years in Dunedin, New Zealand, followed by two years in Perth, Scotland, where he met his wife, Sandy. He returned to the U.S. to do a third residency in Lexington, Kentucky. He then moved to Oswego, New York, where he practiced as an anesthesiologist for nearly twenty-five years. After a short time as Chief of Anesthesiology at Adirondack Medical Center, in Lake Placid, New York, John and Sandy retired to Big Sky, Montana. John is an avid golfer, skier, and as anyone who knows him can tell you, a fine storyteller.

Steve Abbott is a Colorado native, and lives with his wife Adrienne in Boulder, Colorado. He graduated from the University of Colorado, where he and John were roommates during their undergraduate years. After over twenty-five years in the computer industry, Steve returned to CU to obtain a Master's degree in English Literature, which turned out to be much more fun than software support. He has since retired and spends his time reading, writing, and trying to play the hammered dulcimer.